Route 66 Dreamer

Michael Lund

BeachhouseBooks

Chesterfield Missouri USA

Route 66 Dreamer

Copyright 2013 Michael Lund

Cover Design by John Lund

ISBN9781596300835 beachhousebooks.com/

Publication date April, 2013

Library of Congress LCCN 2013934866

BeachHouse Books

www.beachhousebooks.com

an Imprint of
Science & Humanities Press
PO Box 7151
Chesterfield, MO 63006-7151
(636) 394-4950

At Home and Away

by Michael Lund

This five-volume novel series chronicles an American family during times of peace and war from 1915 to 2015. The first book, *Route 66 Sweetheart* (2011), was set mostly in and around Rutherford, New Jersey, during the 1930s, where a young woman who traces her ancestry back to the early New World settlement of Nantucket comes to maturity in the Depression. This second installment (2012) features the Missouri-born son of a Swedish immigrant who, in the early 1940s, pursues his dreams of American success in a land haunted by the prospect of approaching war. However, in both books some family members move away to distant countries and unexpected challenges.

The action in the third volume (2013) will take place primarily in the Midwest during the 1950s and '60s, but characters in that book also journey far from home and the comforts of a familiar world. The fourth volume (2014) will follow another generation of family members, this time from Missouri to Southeast Asia and back again. In the final installment of the saga (2015) their children travel from Virginia and North Carolina through Europe and the Middle East to understand their identity in a multi-national community.

Route 66 Dreamer Acknowledgements

by Michael Lund

2012

More than ten years ago, when BeachHouse Books accepted my first book, *Growing Up on Route 66*, I felt I was luckiest writer alive. *Route 66 Dreamer* is my tenth book in this series, so I should be ten times as happy today. I am.

Dr. Bud Banis, founder of Science & Humanities Press and its imprint, BeachHouse Books, has been generous in his support of my literary efforts, wise in bringing books to life in the fast-changing publishing industry, and—perhaps most remarkable in this age--uninterested in promoting himself over the service he provides. I am pleased to be in the debt of such a man.

I owe Jim Shifflett thanks yet again for reading an early version of this manuscript, pointing out inconsistencies as well as simply awkward writing, and offering many suggestions for revision that I have taken. John Lund composed the cover, using family photographs and knowledge of those who inspired this story. An artist in his own right, his vision more than complements my own.

At the end of this volume is a song, "Dream On, My Heart," composed by my father, the man who inspired this book. I did not find it among his papers until after I had completed the manuscript, but was pleased that my fictional portrait is consistent with his musical creation.

As always, any errors in fact or inconsistencies of narration in the pages that follow are attributable solely to the author.

For Louis Harold Lund
and Carl A. Lund

Prologue: Fast Fingers

During one of his regular Wednesday lunches with me at the retirement home's dining room, my son asked about his father's withdrawal toward the end of his life, after he'd retired and we'd taken a few of those trips I'd dreamed of to other parts of the world. I responded by asking Curtis, "Do you remember the shoe-tying contests you used to have with your father?"

"Of course, I remember those contests. You know, Nana," he said, leaning close, "that I was the fastest gun in the West." He laughed, partly because it was a good memory but also because it hadn't been at all clear which of the three men in my family was the fastest. (No one considered the possibility that I might have been faster than all three.)

"What was it that got you three started in that silliness?" I asked, more aware than he suspected of how it had begun. They'd all been watching *Have Gun Will Travel* and *Gunsmoke*, their father recording the number of deaths over the course of a season (he did love to tabulate!) and the boys thrilled by adventure.

Every Saturday night the shows came on television one after the other, seen by pretty much everybody in our nation. I pretended to enjoy them, too, but usually concentrated more on my knitting once the others were caught up in watching.

"Dad was always competitive," Curtis explained, as if he were telling me something I hadn't learned during those years when we were first married, before his sons were born. "It didn't matter if it was alphabetizing index cards, adding up the prices of grocery items, buttoning your shirt--he'd always turn it into a contest."

"Sports, too," I agreed. "He wanted to be the best hitter, the fastest runner, the ping-pong champion at the Lacy family reunions."

"What made him that way, I wonder?"

"I'm not sure," I pretended. "He did say he had to be scrappy as a kid growing up in some tough neighborhoods and moving all the time. If you weren't good at games, you'd get picked on . . . or ignored. You also didn't didn't get the girls if you couldn't excel! And Oscar wanted to win the prettiest, the smartest, the most popular."

"Well, he certainly did that!" This boy has always been good with compliments!

"But didn't the shoe-tying business start when you were watching Westerns a lot? That's where the showdown came from."

"You mean 'shoe-down,' according to Dad. Now that I think about it, he made a provocative announcement at breakfast one morning: 'I can outgun any man in the house'"

2

"That sounds like him. When you boys sat down at the table, he issued the challenge."

We lived in a conventional two-bedroom house in Fairfield, Missouri, then, with living room, dining room, and kitchen in a row across the front, two bedrooms behind them and two small rooms in the attic.

"Louis and I thought he meant using our Wild Bill Hickok and Roy Rogers pistols. We each had twin sets with holsters, and we'd had such contests before."

"Right. He used that .22 pistol of his, which he'd bought in Indianapolis, working for the Navy during the war. He removed the cylinder, but what did he have for a holster?"

"Oh, he was braggadocious! Stuck his gun in his pants and said he was still the fastest."

I chuckled. He'd made other boasts about the gun in his trousers, but that's not something you tell your son, even if, like Curtis, he's old enough to be on Medicare. "But that morning it wasn't guns he was talking about, was it? It was shoes."

"Right. As I remember, he was getting up early for his first class those days and dressed in the semi-darkness. Feeling his fingers fly convinced him no one could beat him."

"I was already in the kitchen making coffee and setting out the breakfast things--your Wheaties and Cheerios, the bread, butter, and jelly for toast. I didn't witness his dexterity."

"Carol paid no attention to the bragging, but we weren't willing to let the boast go untested. So, that evening--and on quite a few other evenings-- we faced off in the living room."

I sighed dramatically. "Ah, and I had to be the one to say 'Go for your guns!'"

"That I don't remember. But I do recall specific rules: the laces had to lie straight out to the side in starting, your hands had to be at least six inches away from the tips, the bow at the end had to have both loops and no gap in the knot."

Their father loved rules, precise requirements for behavior. Part of it was because his mother had always been strict; but it was also the tenor of the times, the Cold War years when vigilance and attention to detail meant--or so we believed--the survival of the free world. We were at peace after Korea, but always preparing for the next, inevitable conflict.

"What I also remember," Curtis went on, smiling, "was that Dad embellished a scenario for the fastest shoe contests, every night adding goofy elements to the ritual."

I laughed with him. "Oh, he loved to do that, didn't he! He always was the dreamer."

"He'd act like an announcer and say, 'A stranger walks into Plato's Saloon and puts his gun on the bar.' Then switching voices: "'Any man thinks he's as good as me better be ready to back it up.'" Of course, it was his shoe, not a gun, Oscar set on the coffee table.

"You were always better than Louis at taking up the story line. Your brother just wanted to get on with the contest, enter the results in the record book, calculate the odds for different methods." Curtis also liked to keep the pretty girl in the picture.

"So, Dad, as the Marshal, declared, 'I'm not saying I'm better than you, Stranger, but there'll be no gun play in here tonight--especially with ladies present." The other guy (still Dad) would growl, 'Mister, if you're asking me to pick up my gun, you'd better take up yours, too.'"

It was comical, of course, because then I'd say "go"--or whatever I said--and one grown man and two silly teenagers, crouched over their shoes, would grab their shoelaces and flip them, cross them, tuck them, pull them, throw up their hands to declare victory.

"You'd have to be the judge, wouldn't you, Nana, watching to be sure no one got a head start and then inspecting the tie to see that it was valid?"

"I did, but, pretty soon, with the rules in place, that wasn't a hard task."

More than shoe-tying was simple back then, for us. We had goals--work hard, save, prepare for the future. That framework was understood by the whole community. America was growing, becoming the most powerful free nation on earth, responsible for opposing the authoritarian regimes of the Soviet Union and Red China. It was Matt Dillon versus the outlaw.

Especially after Sputnik in 1957, science and math teachers had to keep us in front by improving education. We didn't count on girls like our daughter, Carol, who turned out to be the scientist of our children. But all of them were supposed to do as we--later known as the Greatest Generation--had done: stop the spread of tyranny.

Curtis seemed to be thinking about this larger context as well. "Life got a bit more complicated for us, though, after the years of shoe-tying. We got into the '60s. All the rules came into question. For example, the war I was in far away from home didn't have clear boundaries of good and evil, enemy and ally, black and white."

"Yes, and the division of 'black and white' back home was turning out to be more complicated than we'd thought--the Civil Rights movement. And almost at the same time, the cherished distinctions between men and women turned into the 'battle of the sexes.'"

"Yeah. Dad was never comfortable with all those changes. Oh, he didn't do badly overall. Having taught all those years at an engineering college, with mostly male students, he wanted the categories clear, the tasks straightforward, goals well-defined."

"Well," I said, pushing back from the table and reaching for my cane. "Maybe now you can see why, as the world became even more complicated toward the end of the century, he retreated into a private world, to an ideal realm associated with Route 66, the American Dream."

Until somewhere in what he liked to call, jokingly, "the youth of old age," Curtis' father had relished the fight, whether it was boys competing for a girl, teams battling over a trophy, nations at war--so long as the rules were clear and the rewards noble. He inherited that combative attitude from his parents, an Ozark farm girl turned school teacher and an immigrant Swedish craftsman.

As we came to a new millennium, however, the world went topsy-turvy. Being the fastest got complicated when sandals and flip-flops were accepted footwear; if someone had special shoelaces that magnified ability; by women (having worn such different shoes all their lives) having to be given extra considerations.

Bless him, he tried. But, in the end, all he wanted was to be the best and to win the prettiest. For many, many years, that's what he did. And it's what I'm going to talk about now.

In his retirement, Oscar Lindbloom came to know a trained master of martial arts. Sergeant Major Willie Smith (Ret.) and his wife moved in next door to the Lindblooms after the Jensons-- like a lot of the friends they'd made over the years in Fairfield--moved to Arizona.

"There are two ways to defeat an opponent," Willie explained one afternoon, raising his right hand like a hatchet, sharp edge down. Oscar had crossed backyards to inspect his neighbor's vegetables. He never saw the value of home gardening himself, but liked to hear Willie's stories.

Once a pretty good welterweight, Oscar took up a defensive pose. "We're just demonstrating here, right?" He was well aware of his friend's thick fingers, the scarred knuckles. He also knew Willie had seen combat in his native country, and in World War II.

Willie ignored him. "You can make a direct cut, which will end the encounter." He slashed his hand at Oscar's arm, suggesting it would be broken or rendered useless. Of course, he stopped just short of contact. Oscar had not flinched.

"Alternatively, you can execute a glancing blow." He angled a mock swing in a slant across

Oscar's elbow. "Your opponent will continue fighting, unaware of the internal damage that has been done."

"And he'll do more harm to himself?"

As usual, his friend only stared at him.

Willie was Chinese. Escaping from the Japanese at Nanking as a boy, he had made his way to Shanghai, Honolulu, Toronto, and then Oakland. He enlisted after Pearl Harbor and retired from the Army with thirty-five years of service. Oscar had learned that what physical skills Willie possessed were exceeded by his mental gifts of control and concentration.

"I guess, then," Oscar conceded, "I'll try to take the direct blow in our next encounter."

Willie's lesson in martial arts training lingered in Oscar's mind. Reminiscing in his study that evening, he recalled his fistfight with "Tank" Thompson many years earlier, when he was growing up Salinas, Kansas. He'd always viewed that encounter as pivotal in his history. Now he wondered if he'd misunderstood its significance.

Oscar had been escorting the girl many agreed was the prettiest in town to the Saline County Fair. He knew that Diana Light would never be his ideal mate--that woman had to be closer in transcendent beauty to Hollywood stars like Gretta Garbo or Claudette Colbert. But, new to this town and ready for a fresh start, he saw her as an attractive enough prospect.

Diana had asked Oscar for help in the biology class they were both taking. He suspected he was just one more boy she wanted in her circle of admirers, an unknown who seemed confident and assertive. So, he tested her interest with the suggestion she learn more about living creatures-- and perhaps reproductive systems--at the fair.

"Where you going with my girl, Squarehead?" Tank asked, stepping directly into their path outside one the tents. Mark Thompson, whose father ran a farm equipment store, anchored the high school football team's front line with a vengeance. Someone had connected his powerful body with the British Mark I tank from World War I, and Mark was "Tank" from then on. He was also a champion heavyweight wrestler, but much more feared in vacant lot brawling.

"Well, hello, Quasimodo. Aren't you getting ready to appear on stage . . . somewhere." Oscar waved his hand down the row that included sword swallowers, fire eaters, giants, and midgets. He guessed Tank wouldn't know who Quasimodo was, but assumed--correctly--that he would feel the insult.

Tank didn't especially dislike Oscar, though he followed the convention of teasing children whose parents had accents. And he had become irritated that fall with Diana's repeated rejection of his requests for her company.

Tank was also frustrated after paying to see the "Tattooed Dancing Lady" ("Tattooed" was code, he believed, to say that she would appear nude). She had danced around Tank, but kept all her clothes on. So, when he burst through the tent's doors, he was ready to take out his anger on the closest target. Oscar's smiling face, with smiling Diana's arm in his, would do just fine.

Oscar had always felt he had to equal his father in skill (the rifle demonstration) and endurance (Carl worked from dawn to dusk). So, looking at the angry man in front of him, he asked himself one more time if he was his father's son.

His mother, of course, always told him he was not to get into fights. His hands were to be preserved for playing the piano, drawing with fine ink pens, turning the pages of rare and valuable books. He would grow up to be the scholar, musician, or author that she, raised on a remote Missouri farm, could never have become herself. He was also his mother's son.

An only child cannot be what two parents want unless they agree. Carl and Sallie did not.

Like his father, Oscar had a slender build, and one might think he would duck punches or duck out of sight if threatened. But he was quick with his feet and his fists. Moving from little town to little town over the last half dozen years, he'd learned that taking on the first boy to challenge him was the way to acceptance, even if he lost that scrap.

Oscar called Tank "Quasimodo" because he believed Diana, who loved to read romantic tales about misfits and outlaws, would understand the reference. But to himself he thought "Terkoz."

Terkoz was the chief enemy of the young Tarzan in Edgar Rice Burroughs' classic adventure tale. Oscar had devoured all the books he could find by that prolific author after discovering *Tarzan of the Apes*, *Return of Tarzan*, and *Son of Tarzan* in the Lincoln Center Public Library several years earlier. He often fantasized about being that bizarre combination of civilized European white man and primordial beast of the jungle.

"Humph," grunted Tank and swung a huge fist at Oscar.

What happened next had been played out in Oscar's mind many times, though the opponent varied as it had in Tarzan's case. The twelve-year-old in Africa, who'd been raised by apes, battled a gorilla in the cabin his dead father built, discovering by accident the function of a hunting knife. A few years older, Tarzan broke the neck of a lioness using a full nelson he'd learned wrestling with males in his tribe. And in hand-to-hand combat, he vanquished Terkoz, who was carrying off Jane, the woman who would become Tarzan's wife.

Oscar had imagined winning the favor of a beautiful girl, defending her and her honor with an act of heroism. In such cases his hand speed and a strength surprising in someone so slender would be his advantage.

Tank was bigger and stronger than Oscar, and nearly as quick. But he was a wrestler, not a boxer. He won fights by closing with his opponent and quickly or slowly overpowering them. Oscar knew he would likely lose this fight if his rival got a hold on him. And, terribly nearsighted, he couldn't afford to lose his glasses in a scuffle.

So, he slipped the roundhouse right (though it grazed his shoulder), stepped off on his left foot, and threw a vicious left hook into Tanks' midsection. The big man grunted and leaned forward. Then, in a move he'd been successful with against boys his own size, Oscar completed the combination with a right uppercut to the jaw.

Meanwhile, Diana did what a desirable, self-centered girl should do in such circumstances: covered her mouth with the extended fingers of one hand and stepped back to see who would win her attentions as a prize. She expected it to be Tank.

Oscar understood Diana, but couldn't waste time measuring her character right now. He was hoping he could dodge Tank long enough for others to intervene.

The fight, however, was already over. For all the mass and strength of his body, Tank, it turned out, had a glass jaw. No one had ever had the courage to test it until now, but the one solid cross toppled him into the fairground dust.

Surprised but satisfied, Oscar offered Diana his arm and continued her lessons in biology. At the same time, he wondered if his father would be disappointed that he'd been in a fight or proud that he'd won. In either case, he knew there was much to fear from his mother because he was pretty sure he had broken his wrist . . . again.

He'd always thought this fight--and the second encounter they would have later that fall-- were key factors in his decision to be a scientist and to his long, successful career as an academic. Fifty years later, however, weighing Willie Smith's ideas about how to defeat a martial arts opponent, he wondered if Tank's first blow to his shoulder was in the end more significant.

Even later, nearing the end of his life, he would come to think it was Edgar Rice Burroughs who had delivered the most destructive punch of all. But, he concluded, if had fallen victim to an illusion of his physical prowess, it helped him discover the intellectual strength that was his true gift. Of course, his self-awareness did not come without some predictable backsliding.

Oscar's first wrist fracture had come a few years earlier in Clay Center, Kansas, where he fell from the side of the courthouse. But he remembered losing his hold that time less vividly than feeling the grip a girl had taken on his privates. And eventually he came to realize that injuries to his thinking may have occurred at her hands as well as in his fight with Tank.

Fifteen-year-old Babs McCauley, one of six children who seemed to act independently of parental or other control, had made a project of introducing Oscar to ways of the world she had picked up on her own. "You're good at school," she once told him. She was working the red yo-yo Oscar's father had made for him. "Tell me: does f-o-n-y spell a word?"

He laughed and looked across the playground. "You're thinking of phony--with p-h, not f."

"Ah, I see." She was throwing the yo-yo down and snapping it back up in time with the chewing of her gum. At least, he assumed it was gum. "Well, is P-h-a-u-s-t-i-a-n correct?"

"Faustian? Like the legendary wizard?"

"I don't know what it means. I just heard someone . . . someone on the radio say it."

"Well, that's spelled with an f, not a p-h, at the beginning." Oscar had read Goethe's classic play as well as the more familiar English version by Marlowe. He was surprised Babs had picked up on the name. He was also fascinated by the energy with which she worked the yo-yo, flinging it down and catching it on the return in the palm of her hand with a firm slap--smack!

She looked off in the distance with a funny smile and asked, "Well, is p-h-u-c-k a word?"

He eyed her closely. She didn't look at him, but concentrated on putting the yo-yo to sleep-- that is, letting it spin at the end of its string for a few moments before she would give it that sharp pull that would bring it up to her hand--smack!

"Not the way you're spelling it."

Oscar knew how babies are made. Not only had it been explained by his grandparents on the farm when they were breeding pigs, but he'd seen male dogs chasing and catching female dogs more than once.

"Um-hm," said Babs. She swung the sleeping yo-yo back and forth in front of her like a pendulum. Oscar's eyes followed it this way and that. "You sure? I need help with vocabulary. I don't want to stay after school and have to talk with Mr. Springer." The principal was famous for his use of the paddle.

"You're thinking of . . . another word like that . . . like what you spelled."

Babs let the sleeping yo-yo swing out from her body and back, putting her feet wider apart so the toy disappeared under her dress and then reemerged on an arc stretching out toward Oscar. Then she spun around and leaned forward at the waist. Oscar saw the string crease the back of her dress as the yo-yo rose up at him.

"You wanna' have some p-h-u-n?" she asked over her shoulder.

He looked across the playground, wondering if others were watching them. "I think maybe you need to give my yo-yo back now."

She turned around, snapping the yo-yo up into her fist--smack! "Take your toy, then."

Grabbing his outstretched hand, she closed his fingers over the yo-yo. Then she stepped closer to him and, with the hand that had just deposited the yo-yo, reached down and gave his crotch a firm squeeze. "Compared to playing with a yo-yo," she whispered, "it's p-h-a-n-t-a-s-t-i-c-a-l!" And then, laughing, she ran back to the school building.

It took him a few minutes to realize: 1) that he was drastically uninformed about some very important matters involving boys and girls; 2) that Babs had not hurt him--in fact, her grip had been expertly snug; and 3) that it was tobacco he smelled on her breath. Smack times three!

This girl of surprises had also been present when he broke his wrist that first time. Tom Daily

had started a competition by jumping the gap--
"Superman!"--between his house's back porch
and the shed where the family kept chickens.
Then he promised to loan his wooden Popeye
figure to whoever took the biggest dare. Babs
skated the length of 15th Street behind old man
McCort's Model T.

Somewhere in his 90s, this famous resident
motored around town at fifteen miles per hour
every afternoon from 3:00 to 4:00, oblivious to
pedestrian traffic, road signs, and other vehicles.
Since everyone knew it would happen, his Motel
T had a miraculously clear path. Daring kids like
Babs sometimes grabbed onto his rear bumper in
a crouched position and hitched a ride as long as
their skates stayed buckled and he avoided
potholes.

"Hey, Oscar, your turn," claimed Judy Martin
when he met them on his way back from a piano
lesson. "I just climbed the supports of the bridge
over the river."

Oscar had to retrieve a golf ball Sven
Nordquist had placed three stories up the
courthouse east wall before he went off to play
basketball at the University of Kansas in
Lawrence.

"Let me see the Popeye," he asked, in part to
stall for time. The wooden figure sat on a rolling
platform and revealed his spinach-fueled strength
by leaning forward and back to pound a bell with

18

his sledge hammer. The faster he was pulled, the harder he pounded.

"Yours for a week, Oscar," repeated Tom. "Just get the ball off the ledge."

"We'll create a diversion," said Gene. "Put two lit cherry bombs in the bottom of the trash can out front of the court house and cover them with loose newspaper. As soon as you hear someone call 'fire,' you climb."

Oscar turned Popeye this way and that, studying his oddly muscular forearms and nonexistent biceps. At the same time he discretely scanned the faces of the others. From their glances at each other (especially Babs'), he suspected they would stay hidden and quiet, leaving him uncertain when to make the attempt. It was quite likely a set-up.

"Let's go," he said, swinging one leg over the seat of his bicycle. Two things gave him confidence: one with good reason; the other was a fantasy.

Until he was nine, the Lindblooms had lived in Jefferson City. When he could escape his mother, Oscar loved to climb the cliffs made by rivers and in the building of roads. The solid stone courthouse would be less treacherous than porous and crumbly Missouri limestone.

Oscar's other inspiration was John Carter of Mars, like Tarzan, an Edgar Rice Burroughs character. Oscar was intrigued by the commoner from earth who becomes a prince on Mars. The lighter atmosphere and lesser gravity of the red planet gave the Virginia-born Carter the ability to leap higher, run faster, and lift heavier objects than natives of that other world.

His mother disapproved of the Carter books. Finding in his room one day *The Gods of Mars*, second in Burroughs' series, she told him to return it to the library immediately. "I don't want you reading anything about war," she said. "You're not ever to be a soldier." His father, who had served in the Swedish military, agreed. Oscar understood but read the books in secret.

When he studied the Clay Center Courthouse wall up close, he felt more confident than when he'd accepted the challenge. The rough stone provided many places to step and to hold. He also heard Babs whisper to Tom that this was too easy ("but maybe I'll get a good look up his dress!"). His only worry was not seeing his goal clearly, as, extremely nearsighted, he had worn glasses since he was six.

Oscar also adopted a mental strategy that kept his progress steady: he stared at the ledge above him as intently as John Carter--supposedly dead outside an Arizona cave--had gazed upward toward the planet of war in *Under the Moons of Mars*. Where that fictional hero heard an audible snap and felt a brief loss of consciousness before finding himself naked on Martian soil, Oscar Lindbloom heard a boy call out "fire" and then blocked out all thought but to climb.

John Carter learned quickly that "springing to his feet" from a prone position on Mars meant flying three yards into the air because of lesser gravity. In order to walk without bounding along in huge strides, he had to train his earthly muscles all over again, like an infant.

Imagining himself climbing to rescue Deja Thoris (Carter's beloved Martian princess) with sure grip and powerful legs, Oscar moved steadily and easily up the stone face of the building. He squinted to locate handholds and the ball. In a few moments, his hand closed on the round object on the ledge in front of him.

On the way down he interpreted the sound of an exploding cherry bomb as a green Martian firing a radium bullet and jumped to what he believed to be the safety of the (Martian) ground only fifteen feet below him.

When he arrived home, hugging his arm to his stomach, he told his mother that he'd wrecked his bike. (He thought to himself that he had "phallen.") She took the strap to him anyway. About that reality he had never been confused; but he also began to realize that he would soon have to free himself of her gravity.

The courthouse accident didn't occur while Oscar was, as he claimed, "at piano practice," but on the way home. Yet it was during the time he'd announced he would be "at practice." Blurring the startings and stoppings of music lessons, or the exact beginnings and endings of work shifts, allowed him a bit of free time, otherwise hard to extract from his mother's strict supervision. Sallie Lindbloom, neé Bahr, believed her son was a genius and was determined that no accident or deliberate act would prevent his achieving distinction.

His first piano teacher, Miss Jenson, felt a similar conviction. This boy, who seemed to know a lot about musicians and musical history, had a good ear and a feel for melody. His long fingers and exceptional dexterity suggested he was the student for whom she had longed, the future concert performer.

"Oscar," she instructed him, "it's not just your hands that make music; it's also the stories in your head. You must fill yourself with dreams."

He had plenty of dreams, both from his own desires and from his reading. Determined to be at the top of each new class he entered as he moved around the state in those Depression years, he consumed all the books he could get his hands on, including a single (but gigantic) one-volume encyclopedia his mother had bartered for with a neighbor moving west to start his life over in a new place.

"Do you think of other scenes and adventures when you play?" Oscar asked Miss Jenson. She looked old enough to have done many things but was so feeble in body that he couldn't envision what memories had the strength to dance in her mind.

"Oh, dear, yes! My father studied in Italy under the great Busoni. And later he played for orchestras across Europe. I traveled with him . . . "

Her thoughts trailed off, and Oscar studied the first movement of Shostakovich's Concerto No. 2 in F major, imagining (he didn't know why) a scene from Gogol's "The Overcoat," Akaky begging the authorities to help him recover his lost garment.

With the music before him, he moved his hands over keys, not making a sound, but practicing the fingering. His reach was more than an octave and his touch easily rested on black keys, the white strips between them. What would it be like to be a world famous musician, treated as royalty at concert halls and social gatherings? He would wear fine clothes, dance with elegant women, smoke cigars and drink brandy among powerful ministers of state.

Oscar's ideas of Europe came from reading novels by Sir Walter Scott and Alexander Dumas, the courts and politics of a previous age. He paid little attention to the realities of Hitler's rise in Germany, Fascist movements in Italy and Spain. That was a world his father had left behind and one his mother felt had betrayed America. So, his destiny, according to his parents, lay in a great homeland of opportunity and plenty.

Miss Jenson interrupted his reverie. "These hands you see, they have taken me all over the world." She held them up, her fingers still straight and lean, the nails trimmed close.

"You mean you played in many places?"

"Not just played in, but created. When I performed the compositions of Mozart and Listz and Ravel, the cities of Vienna, of Paris, of Florence, rose up around me wherever I was. I heard the people speaking, I lived among them. And you shall do so, as well, my young friend. But first you must practice, practice, practice. Let's return to those études."

Oscar's second teacher, who would become a friend, was decidedly more down-to-earth than Miss Jenson. Harold Lewis, assistant professor of music at Salinas Wesleyan College, took a few private students each semester in addition to those enrolled in his classes. Sallie had pleaded with him to let Oscar audition, and Professor Lewis accepted him immediately.

Even after Oscar broke his wrist in the fight with Tank, the teacher said he could continue on the same schedule, but a lot of the following two months would be spent on music theory. It was clear he saw talent--and maybe something else--in this eager boy.

Coming onto the campus every week gave Oscar the feeling that he was gaining in maturity and poise. And especially after he became known as a David who brought down Goliath, he was convinced he had sufficient experience and confidence to pursue relationships with girls on his own terms. However, one brief encounter with a coed there revealed that his understanding of romance was less complete than he had thought.

Sitting on a bench outside the professor's studio, he heard someone say, "I haven't seen you here before." An attractive young woman, with some notebooks hugged to her chest, was standing before him. "I'm Carol."

In the room behind him another student was practicing a long, involved piece. Oscar thought he or she must be getting ready for a recital. "Oh, hello, hi, I'm Oscar. Yes. I started two months ago. Well, not just started playing the piano, but taking lessons here. I've been studying for. . . several years. But we don't have our own piano, and so I have to practice . . . "

He didn't want to explain that his father had built him a wooden keyboard. It made no sound but the action was excellent. Looking at Carol's expensive clothes, including an elegant pair of pumps, he was sure she had her own piano.

"Well, and I broke my wrist . . . in an accident, so I have books to read about music."

"I see." She touched his cast lightly. "You're not a Wesleyan student, then, are you?" She glanced down the hall, empty at the moment because it was after the last class of the day. She also studied his clothes, an outfit made by his mother that he usually wore at Hedd's. The one sleeve was rolled up.

"No, . . . no. I will be . . . or I'll be in college next year. I'm not sure where I'll go. Probably to Lawrence or maybe Gustavus Adolphus . . . "

He realized he was rambling, but her attention was unsettling. She had sat down on the bench and turned toward him, her face closer to his than he would have expected from a stranger. He regretted mentioning the Lutheran college, as it would show he was Swedish. Well, and perhaps religious.

She slid closer on the bench, possibly because they might have trouble hearing each other over the piano inside the studio. "Oh, I wish I could have gone there! But Daddy didn't want me to be so far away. Of course, they're pretty strict there, like St. Mary's." This was a Catholic school for women in Salinas.

"I like Professor Lewis; he's so . . . knowledgeable." Actually, he felt his teacher was sometimes distant, almost uninterested in his playing. He heard Oscar practice his exercises, told him to be more precise in this spot and that,

26

said he must watch the timing, gave him more dull assignments. "But I don't want just to study music. I'm interested in lots of subjects-- philosophy, mathematics, science. I plan to . . . to do well."

She studied his expression closely, as if there were some secret she might read there. He hoped his wire-rimmed glasses made him look older and more scholarly. "I bet you're the first to go to college in your family, aren't you? You want to see fine art, go to plays, read poetry."

"Well, yes . . . I'm an only child, so . . . "

She leaned closer, her head tilted, and whispered. "Have you ever . . . have you read *Lady Chatterley's Lover*? It's been banned, you know."

"No, I . . . I've heard about it, though. It's controversial, isn't it?"

She looked up and down the hall again. "I have a copy," she whispered, patting her bundle of school material. "You can't imagine the things it describes . . . the love scenes."

"Oh?" Oscar's brain wasn't working too well. She had put a hand on his shoulder and tucked her head down so that blonde curls fell over one side of her face. He could smell the freshness, the sweetness, of shampoo.

"Where do you go," she whispered even more softly, "after, um, your lesson?"

He decided not to admit that he worked at a shoe store. "Oh, I . . . usually head over to the library . . . to read."

She lifted her head so that her lips were beside his ear. "Maybe I'll see you there sometime. I . . . I do a lot of . . . reading." She jumped up and walked swiftly down the hall.

It was possible that he'd imagined it, but he felt almost positive that, when Carol whispered that she might see him, her tongue had flicked out and softly touched his ear.

After that day, Oscar went to the library for many weeks following each lesson, but never saw "Carol." He had no idea how to look for her, even if he'd had the courage. But, having had a taste of sensations he had not felt elsewhere, he sought out other such contact.

Chapter Four: Belt

Whether Oscar's account of the bike's slipping on loose gravel back in Clay Center was true or a fabrication hadn't mattered to his mother. She punished him for injuring the precious body she believed destined for great things. So after the fight with Tank he told the truth (more or less) about breaking his wrist a second time. His forthrightness marked an important stage in breaking free from his domineering mother.

"But I had to defend a lady," he declared dramatically. "We were at the fair, and it wouldn't have gone well with me if I'd let him insult her."

Oscar's father said nothing, as was his custom in such situations. Oscar never told his peers that it was his mother, not his father, who disciplined him. She took Carl's razor-sharpening belt from a hook inside the bathroom door and wielded it with a fury that would have surprised anyone but the two men in her family. And, until the move to Salinas, Oscar submitted.

His arm in a cast up to the elbow on the day after the fight with Tank, he knew what his mother planned to do once Carl left to attend a Lindbloom family gathering in Assyria. She'd let him go to bed the previous night without the confrontation both knew would come. Before she could begin her tirade, however, he announced,

"You can give me chores, or make me pay the doctor, or forbid my going out, but you may not get the belt."

His mother, red-faced, stared at him. In the last year he'd grown taller and filled out. But it was the look in his eyes more than his grown body that stopped her. (He would have liked to believe something like the scar on Tarzan's forehead, which grew red when he was enraged, was visible on his own face.)

She said, "I've told you--no fighting. You know where it got your Uncle John."

Sallie's brother had been famous for getting into scrapes as a boy and as a young man. His frustrated young bride finally agreed to his volunteering for the war in France with a hope that the battlefield would finally tame him. It did. An invalid since Ypres, John had been looked after by that wife, a saint as far as Sallie was concerned. Agnes ran a diner two blocks from the capitol in Jefferson City and next door to the little shotgun house where she tended to her husband.

Oscar's father, for whom military service had been compulsory, was as adamant as Sallie that their son avoid becoming, even briefly, a soldier. In this case, Oscar's poor eyesight might be a blessing. What combat experiences Carl had had in the old country, Oscar would not learn until the eve of the Second World War, when he himself faced induction.

For at least a minute, Oscar confronted his mother in the hall outside the bathroom. He explained again that his wrist was still fragile from the first break in Clay Center, so it was, he claimed, a freak accident that injured him.

The bone had, in fact, been badly set. And it would turn out that setting it a second time only increased the irregularity. Throughout his life, Oscar's left wrist bone was twice the size of his right one and his manual mobility was restricted.

As the standoff continued, the boy, who could not have known what his mother was thinking, imagined how poor Pip in *Great Expectations* felt at the mercy of The Tickler. Dickens' classic tale had been required reading in his last year at Clay Center, and the fictional boy's rise to fortune and respectability had thrilled Oscar.

Finally, his mother put her hands on her hips and demanded, "What will you tell Professor Lewis?"

"I guess the same thing we told Miss Jenson, Mother."

Oscar knew she was asking a rhetorical question. In fact, he had his own ideas about the musical future he intended at one point to discuss with his teacher. Rather than pursuing the classical career foreseen by his mother, Oscar dreamed of joining one of the Big Bands and touring the country with Billie Holiday or Bessie Smith.

"Well, you ask him next week for some of those one-handed exercises she had you use, though we won't get much return for what we have to pay him," said his mother. "And today you'd better stay late at the shoe store so you get your work done . . . with that sling."

She gestured at his arm and turned toward the kitchen. Over her shoulder she concluded, "Mr. Hedd, you know, can find other boys who want to earn money and help their families."

This was a constant theme at their Park Street home. The Depression had been especially hard on immigrant families with no roots in the community. After the market crashed and banks began to close, the Lindblooms were forced to leave Jefferson City and move from town to town looking for construction jobs. Rather than follow Route 66 across Texas as many did, they returned to the region where Carl had lived earlier.

Separation from family--her parents and two married brothers--had been painful for Sallie. Even with their changing locations, she lobbied hard for visits to Missouri whenever possible. And Carl had agreed that one would come this year around the Christmas holidays.

After some years of irregular employment, the Lindblooms settled in Salinas, in part because Carl had relatives in the small Swedish community nearby. Their frugal farming meant they had food to share with Carl's family. Throughout their nomad years, Sallie would wash and sew clothes when there was work available. She also managed, in the places that had space, a small kitchen garden.

In each location Carl was ready to take on everything from home construction to cabinetry to lumber cutting. And Oscar, until his education was complete, had to accept work available to a boy his age. He was allowed a small allowance from his earnings and right now was saving for a special trip he wanted to take in the winter.

He told his mother, "Mr. Hedd would expect me to do what I'm supposed to even if I was on crutches!" He generally worked the stockroom for two hours each school day. On Saturdays, he sold shoes and managed the store so his boss could have some time off, though Mr. Hedd often stopped in for an hour or more to make sure Oscar and Betty were working.

"Well, you know your father will want to have dinner when he usually does and then listen to the radio, so don't you be late."

Carl generally pretended to listen to *Flash Gordon, the Kraft Music Hall,* and the *Lux Radio Theater,* but he spent much of his evenings reminiscing about his childhood in Sweden and the girl he left behind there. It was Oscar who imagined himself flying through space, taking a clarinet solo in Woody Herman's band, romancing Joan Crawford. Sallie would sew or read the Bible, not really aware of what either man in her life was thinking.

Though he'd not told either parent, Oscar was planning to skip his senior year and go away to college early. Before that occurred, he wanted to make the most of every opportunity at home. He'd already distinguished himself at different schools in music, art, science, math, and writing. He won an essay contest in his last year at Clay Center with "Plato's Cave and Kansas Plains."

Still more was to be accomplished on the romantic front. Asking Diana Light to the fair had been the happy result of impulse. Now he had the opportunity to do more. At school during the lunch period on Monday, he asked his best friend, Bob, "What's everyone saying?"

"They're saying, even if you have the hammer of Thor, you'd better watch out for Tank, you idiot." He gestured where many on the football team, including the center, were eating.

Oscar scanned the tables where some of the cheerleaders and the drum majorettes were sitting. "Yeah, sure. But the girls, what do they say?"

"Diana says the two of you fought it out for her, and you won." He paused, possibly wishing he'd become the talk of the school himself. "But, if I were you, I'd worry that she was taking advantage of you to bring Tank down a peg. I think she wants him. So, anyway, what are you going to do, now that you've got the attention of the whole class?"

Oscar thought about this. Since coming to Salinas, he'd not made that many friends. His abilities put off some; and he covered an underlying shyness with a studied formality. Bob Peterson, though, whose parents were also Swedish, had sought him out. Because they were both only sons, they had a lot in common.

"It might be that I'll see which other girls are impressed that I knocked Tank out."

"Ha!" laughed Bob. "Having your arm in a cast takes a little of the shine off your glory."

After a pause, he asked, "Can you come over tomorrow and help me milk the goats?" His father kept half a dozen of the difficult creatures in a lot behind their house. Oscar didn't like them, but he was grateful to Bob for taking pains to explain the pecking order in the school and the social structure of the town.

"Sure, after I'm done at Hedd's."

There were advantages to staying away from home a few extra hours this week. His mother had backed down about the belt, but he knew her determination to control his life had not slackened. He would have to continue to fight for his freedom.

Chapter Five: Heavy Hands

Despite this boldness in front of his mother, Oscar worried about what his father, who had said nothing so far about the broken wrist, felt about the fight with Tank.

Carl had advised his son to talk his way out of confrontations whenever possible. But he also told him that, if he knew a situation would come to blows, he should strike first and hit hard. Oscar had wanted his taciturn Scandinavian father to be proud of him, and to show it, as far back as that time when Carl had taught him to shoot.

"Take this spool down the lane there," Carl said to his son that summer day back in Clay Center, handing him a damaged wooden cylinder he had made years previously for Sallie's sewing basket. "Go on past that last tree. Place it right in the middle."

Though his English pronunciation was good, Carl spoke with the customary lilting rhythm of his native speech. Changing the sound of "j" to "y" (jump became yump) was the other most conspicuous reminder of his native tongue

They had walked from their house into the country--a short journey, given the size of Clay Center. The distance Oscar carried the target was probably about 100 feet, the spool's height perhaps an inch and a half. Carl had borrowed a neighbor's Remington 22 to demonstrate for his son. On the way Oscar asked if his father had had a rifle when he was growing up.

"No, they were expensive, now. But my uncle, he would let us borrow his sometimes, for squirrel hunting." Carl lost his mother at the age of twelve and was raised from then on by his older sister, Kristina. After elementary school he went to work in the mines near his home in Bjuv. It was hard times in Sweden then, and, as soon as they were old enough, his older siblings immigrated to America. They joined a small community in Assyria, where Carl and two of his brothers arrived early in the twentieth century.

"You breathe slowly," Carl explained, "but don't hold your breath. If you were taking only one shot, that would be good. But always you want to be ready to fire more than once, steadily, accurately. So, you keep the air coming in and going out, regular."

"Did you learn to shoot in the Army?"

"Yah, I learned to shoot better. That's what they do in armies."

Carl had told his son little about life in the Old Country, though it was clear from the few accounts he did give that he missed the woods, the hills, the winding streams of his boyhood home. The vast empty prairie of Kansas was an alien world, and he'd moved to Missouri in part because the landscape reminded him of his homeland.

"What did you do in the army? Were you in battles?"

"That was a lot of years ago, you know. Now we live in peace, and you are a lucky boy to grow up in a nation that is far away from conflict and where your abilities are recognized."

Oscar had seen his father study his school report cards and the certificates of accomplishment--after, of course, his mother had scrutinized them. But the boy couldn't tell if he had simply met his father's high expectations or exceeded them. The family always spoke matter-of-factly about the achievements of his older, successful Swedish cousins.

"When you were growing up, Dad, did you . . . were there a lot of fights with other boys?"

"Yah, when I was in school there were. But once I went to work, there was no time for such foolishness. We worked hard to save money to come here."

"Did you win the fights you were in?"

A smile spread over Carl's face. "I won my share, but the real fighter in our family was my sister, your Aunt Kristina."

"Really?"

Oscar had only seen his aunt a few times, but he knew she ran a store and grain elevator with her husband in tiny Hallville, Kansas. At that moment, though, he pictured his father's older sister as Swedish film star Gretta Garbo in *Queen Christina.*

"One time Nils and I were being attacked on the way home from school. Every day it was, by older boys."

"They were bigger than you?"

"Yah, they were. And more used to fighting than we were. It was a hard time. We tried to stay away from them, but they were always waiting close to our home. And they would catch us, so we would have to fight. But we lose, until the day Kristina came to our rescue."

Oscar thinks of Gretta Garbo in the final scene of *Queen Christina,* a figurehead on the bow of a boat sailing away from her home country. The wind blows back her hair, and her strong beauty takes his breath away.

"She told the bullies to leave you alone?"

Carl laughed softly. "More than that. She hid in the bushes where Nils and I would pass. When those other boys came along and started to pick a fight, she came out and beat them up. Oh, she beat them up good with her big strong hands! And they never bothered us again."

Oscar recalled the movie Christina, who disguises herself as a man in order to escape the pressures of governing. In a snowstorm she comes to an inn and ends up sharing a bed with Antonio, a Spanish envoy with whom she falls in love.

"She beat them up? How many were there? And how did she do it? Just with her fists?"

Carl sighed and patted him on the shoulder. "Those times are gone, Oscar. Your mother . . . she don't want me to dwell on that part of my life. We all learn to speak English over here and become Americans."

The Lindblooms and others Swedes in Assyria spoke Swedish when they were by themselves, but Sallie insisted Carl use only English at home. The war and the injuries to her brother had soured her on Europe, as it had many Americans.

Oscar knew, though, that late in the fall each year the community in Assyria would quietly observe Gustavus Adolphus day, remembering the great King of Sweden and hero of Protestantism. Sometimes they would sing the national anthem, "Du Gamla, Du Fria" (You Old, Free Nation) and "Hell Dig, Du Hoga Nord" (Hail Thee, Thou Great Northland).

If Carl had tried to teach his son more of such traditions, Sallie must have stopped him early in his childhood. She even put some distance between herself and her own, less educated family from Tuscumbia. Her son would rise above the level of farmer, soldier, carpenter.

"Now you watch, boy, and I will show you what to do." Carl squinted over the rifle barrel, his body still, both hands firm. Oscar saw his father's shortened thumb on his right hand curled over

40

the stock. He pulled the trigger five times, and the spool danced down the road. Each bullet found its mark, all after the first a moving target.

Making sure his glasses were tight on his ears and nose, Oscar then had his turn and did not disappoint his father. As with all feats of skill, he wanted to be the best. So, he followed instructions carefully, concentrated intently, and acted deliberately.

Over the course of that summer, father and son returned to the fields to practice, each time over longer distances and with more targets. They kept the project a secret, of course, from Sallie, who would have connected the use of guns to the sad case of her brother.

Oscar had reason to consider his Missouri uncle and the use of guns later in his life, when Pearl Harbor was bombed. While other young men were rushing to enlist, he weighed the experiences of the previous generation recorded in books and recounted in his presence. His father also finally broke his silence about his experience in the Swedish military.

For the first nine years of his life, he had accompanied his parents many times to his aunt and uncle's little house in downtown Jefferson City. While visitors sometimes directed conversation to John, his wife fielded most of their questions and made responses for her husband. His lungs and respiratory system had been damaged to the point that he spoke only in a whisper and couldn't take enough breath for the littlest exertions.

Oscar noticed that his father was always especially solicitous of his invalid brother-in-law. More than once, the boy observed the two of them had engaged in intimate conversations about their pasts. Over time, seeing his father's somber behavior at Uncle John's, he came to the conclusion that Carl saw no winners in war.

Oscar would find little change in Agnes and John, by the way, when, after college, he came to Jefferson City to look for work. Having, in a sense, run away from home, he instinctively counted on his aunt to help him begin a new life. She didn't disappoint him, not only giving him room and board for a time, but also introducing him to the woman he would one day marry.

In Salinas, though, as a high school junior, Oscar desperately wanted to be John Gilbert to a local Greta Garbo. And he hoped Diana Light would be willing to let him play that role.

Chapter Six: A Delicate Touch

Oscar could move stock with the cast on his broken wrist, if less efficiently than usual. Helping women try on shoes with his arm in a sling, however, was more troublesome. And when Diana showed up with her mother Saturday after lunch, his ability to improvise was challenged.

Betty Devine, who had a crush on him, would have been happy to step in, of course. But Oscar felt more than a salesman's satisfaction in getting customers to buy. There was also a secret, guilty pleasure involved in the process he did not want to relinquish, especially to a girl.

"Oscar," Betty asked him, studying his arm in cast and sling. "Oscar, did you . . . do you think your injury was a sign? A warning?"

He laughed. "Oh, yes. Keep the wrist stiff, whether you're throwing a body punch or aiming for a knockout." He was putting shoes in their boxes back into proper order in the storeroom. She had offered to hold those for which there was not yet a space.

Concern showed on her face. "Not about how to fight, but about why you fight, and what comes of giving in to the desire to . . . to hit someone."

Oscar didn't believe he had a desire to strike, but he knew where this was heading. Betty attended the Baptist church, and the minister there was known for fiery sermons about sin and punishment. He was especially opposed to violence, and many believed he would urge the country to stay out of war, should it break out again in Europe.

"You mean you think I'm going to hell, don't you."

She frowned. "That's something only you can decide. I just think you need to ask yourself why . . . why you fought. You could have hurt Tank. Or you might have been hurt yourself."

He smiled. "Don't you worry, Betty. I can take care of myself. But right now, I'd better take care of our first customers." He'd heard the bell on the door jingle and used the sound as a way to escape further discussion.

Oscar actually liked Betty quite a bit. She was bright and open, friendly, easy to work with. Well, she was attractive also, even though the way she dressed often hid it. At times, he'd imagined going on a date with her, sitting on the porch swing of her parents' home, perhaps kissing those often smiling lips.

But it was clear Betty worried about a tendency to violence in Oscar; and that concern slid easily into fear at his indifference to Jesus. He had admitted once that he had attended the Church of Christ as a child. But he didn't tell her, when the time came back in Clay Center to be baptized, he had held back. When they moved to

Salinas, Oscar told his mother he would go to church only when he felt the need--which had so far turned out to be not at all.

Sallie had a hard time persuading her son to go because his father, who had been raised in a strict Lutheran household, would not accompany her. Carl admitted that he believed in God, that worshipping was a good thing. But he would not tolerate sermons that played on guilt and the occasional emotional outbursts of some members.

Falling back on her belief in her son's gifts, Sallie had decided to focus her demands on his performance at school and with his music. After all, growing up on a farm in rural Missouri, her family had not always been able to attend church. Yet they were all good Christians.

Oscar and Betty found business steady that day at Hedd's, though much of it involved damaged shoes being left for Mr. Larson, who was also employed by local farmers needing their equipment mended. Money was tight, of course, so purchases were rare, except with such people as the Lights.

"Hi," said Diana cheerfully. "Mother, you remember the boy who took me to the fair."

"Of course, dear. You're new at school this year, young man, aren't you?"

"Yes, Mrs. Light. We moved to town in the summer. Now, are you my customer today, or should I bring out some things for Diana?"

"We're both interested in seeing the new styles. There are . . . ah . . . a number of important social events coming up for which we must dress appropriately. Could we see what you have in a dress shoe?"

Oscar moved eagerly to the store room, passing by the less expensive items on the display rack. If he could make a good sale with only one arm, Mr. Hedd would not question his ability to perform regular tasks at the store. Too, there was the exciting prospect of serving Diana.

He thought of Tolstoy's Levin in *Anna Karenina*, fascinated by Kitty Shtcherbatsk putting her "slender feet in their high boots" and skating gracefully. Oscar wanted Diana to slip her small foot into a shoe held by his strong hands.

"These are being worn in Kansas City and Chicago," he told Mrs. Light, holding up a pair of brown shoes. The top had an open strip, exposing a portion of the foot much as a sandal would. The upper tie was made from satin and needlepoint lace. "But," added Oscar, "it was inspired by an Italian designer."

Mr. Hedd had warned Oscar about showing foreign shoes to certain customers, those who might have been concerned at the rise of Fascism in Europe. He had relatives in Germany himself and worried about their welfare. Somehow, Oscar didn't think this would matter with the Lights.

Still, he held a second box under his arm, with the top placed beneath it so the shoes inside were visible; the fancy shoe was not the only choice. He had, however, deliberately chosen something, which, though expensive, had been purchased by several women recently.

Diana's mother put her foot on the slanted front portion of the little bench Oscar was straddling and indicated with a gesture that he should remove the shoe she was wearing and put on the expensive one. Diana waited patiently in the next seat.

When Mrs. Light rose to test the fit, walking away for a moment, Diana winked at Oscar. "I'm not sure I can dance in that shoe," she whispered, straightening one leg in an expensive silk stocking so that it stretched out beside Oscar. "Don't you think I should be able to use my gifts?"

He studied her leg, the calf tensed as she pointed her toes. Current dress style prevented his seeing even as high as her knee. "Ah, yes. And I believe I have just what you need. Would you, um, stand and take a few steps, so I can see the way your ankles bend and . . . ah, how everything moves together."

She walked in the opposite direction from the one her mother had taken, spun on one heel, and returned. He wondered if she knew he was watching her backside, and if she deliberately made it swing the way it did. "You'll have to imagine me waltzing late into the evening. Whatever you find for me has to be strong and flexible enough to last all night long."

Levin and Kitty's love story in *Anna Karenina* is not as steamy as Vronsky's and Anna's. And Oscar, like most young readers, was drawn to the adulterous couple's drama when he read the book over the summer. He remembered especially the scene at the train station where Anna meets the man who will seduce her--but not because of the famously shocking death of a railway guard. Instead, Oscar recalled Vronsky's being thrilled by "the rapid step which bore her rather fully-developed figure with such strange lightness." It would be years before the stability of Levin's marriage became the romantic model for Oscar and his true sweetheart.

"I can picture you dancing," Oscar told Diana, pushing his glasses up on his nose. "In fact, I hear in my mind's ear the music of Vienna; I see couples twirling in the Wilhelm Gause Hofball; I sense the temperature rising as the excitement grows."

Then he rose, smiling. "Those shoes, Mrs. Light, look beautiful on you."

Oscar wasn't at all sure what the daughter would like and didn't want to disappoint her; so he decided to bring as many boxes as he could carry so that she would see variety. Then he would insist she try on any shoe she felt might be right, but not only because he wanted her to leave a satisfied customer.

Oscar predicted that Diana's dress would somehow slip up a little higher than necessary when she placed her foot on the bench. And he felt her toes would not take a straight trajectory into each shoe, but oddly wander toward his left or his right hand. He knew his own fingers, pulling the back of the shoe over her heel, testing the fit over an instep, opening wide to frame the product, would make contact with more than was necessary.

It was all a dance, of course, a cautious, delicate ritual played out in every civilized generation of human history. He doubted that the game he and Diana were playing--of which her mother was quite aware--would lead to anything serious. The exchange with Carol at Salinas Wesleyan had not. But, as he had told his friend Bob, he remained committed to seeing how far his reputation as a giant killer would make him a lady killer at Salinas High School.

Chapter Seven: Milking

Oscar was not keen on milking goats, but he liked his new friend. He also had to admit that it was helpful to know someone who knew the terrain of Salinas High School.

"There's a hay ride in two weeks-- homecoming weekend," Bob told Oscar as they stood on the side of the pen and surveyed the Peterson's small herd. Bob's father had built a simple metal lean-to on his lot and fenced in about an acre of scruffy land to keep his six goats.

"You want to double date?" Oscar offered. "We could ask the Martin sisters."

Bob chuckled. The twins were pleasant but gigantic girls who had been the talk of the school after Jim Turner claimed to have gone skinny dipping with them one hot August night. "I don't know, 'Scar. If Tank shows up with a friend from the football team, I'm not sure I want to have to rescue you."

"Hah! Well, you do have the Hammer of Thor."

Back in September, Bob and Oscar had been swimming on Saturday in the Salinas River west of town. When the sky darkened and a storm approached, Bob said it was time to get out of the water. But Oscar wanted to stay in longer because it was so hot.

"Beware the Hammer of Thor," Bob had commanded, striking a dramatic pose on the river's edge and raising a crooked log he'd picked up from the bank. In the next instant a bolt of lightning lit up the sky, and a clap of thunder shook the air. Ever since, Oscar attributed special powers to his friend.

Oscar studied the goat who had chased him over the fence on his first visit. "I think Betty Devine would like to go. You could ask her, and Tank won't be jealous." Betty's reputation as a good girl restricted her field of potential admirers.

"She is pretty, but she has a crush on you. And I bet you're going to ask Diana? Strike while the iron is hot and all."

"I might, though I'm not sure Mrs. Light will want her classy daughter rolling around in the hay with the son of a carpenter, sawdust in his hair and dirt under his nails."

This was partly a joke, as Oscar was meticulous in keeping his hands clean and fingernails trim. His mother assumed it was so he could play his musical instruments and was pleased. Bob thought it made him look a bit of the dandy, so it was good that Oscar knew how to defend himself.

"I'm not sure Diana's the type to roll around anyway," Bob said. "Ballroom dancing at the country club is more her style. One arm around the waist, the other held away from the body. So," he gestured to the goats, which had crowded together in front of them. "you ready?"

"Sure, but after you."

Oscar let Bob lead the way through the gate. Although their udders were full, the does sometimes took advantage of carelessness to slip past them in search of new things to eat. Grumpy, the largest and most ornery of the herd, seemed to be eyeing Oscar's jacket. She'd gone after the extra large buttons before.

Oscar was reminded of the story of the "Billy Goats Gruff," which his mother read to him when he was a young child. It was irrational, he knew, as all the Peterson goats were female; but being here made him recall the scary troll under the bridge. And, whenever he entered the pen, he couldn't quite shake a vague feeling of anxiety.

Of course, in the traditional tale Sallie told, the goats outsmart the troll. But she added some subtle details to convince her young son that monsters lurked along the road of life, waiting to snatch up the lazy and the foolhardy. Oscar also worried that Grumpy suspected him--troll or not--of planning a goat steak dinner.

"You take Sneezy," Bob said, "and I'll start with Dopey. You don't know what's going on, do you, girl?" He pulled the goat onto the milking stand and lowered the restraining collar on her neck. Checking for dirt or trash on her underside, he found everything clean and began to massage her teats.

52

On Oscar's first visit, Bob had run through all the jokes about squeezing teats the other boys teased him with. (There were other taunts even more unpleasant, but, for a time, he kept quiet about them with his new, more sophisticated friend.) He explained to Oscar that when you milked seven days a week fifty-two days a year, cleaned the animals and their quarters daily, treated for disease and injury more often than you wanted, a life with goats was hardly a titillating experience ("pun intended").

Oscar hadn't taken the jokes seriously. The process of reaching under a goat to grab whatever was hanging down was unrelated to any contact he hoped to have with someone of the opposite sex. If a girl were on all fours, there would be nothing at the back end to wrap your fingers around. And Sneezy, his current companion--who smelled as if she'd rolled in rotten potatoes--was hardly an attractive creature.

"You know," Bob said. "They'll be some kids who go on the hay ride without dates."

"Human kids, not goat ones?"

"Ha. Right."

"But the ones without dates are usually the 'nice' boys and girls who'll want to sing hymns and recite Bible verses. I . . . we . . . need to get a bit more . . . .um . . . experience before we leave high school."

Oscar had told Bob that he planned to attend college next fall, skipping his senior year at Salinas High. At his mother's urging back in Clay Center, he'd already been advanced one grade.

But he didn't look younger than his classmates and had no trouble with schoolwork.

"I don't know. If you stay another year here, you'll be the king of the school and can get any girl you want."

For all his bravado, Oscar hadn't "gotten" any girl so far in his young life. He regularly entertained elaborate fantasies of romantic encounters with beautiful women. They started tamely and ended in frantic . . . well . . . frantic rolling around in the hay. But the real girls who appeared receptive to his charms fell short of these ideals. In the few situations where opportunity arose, his ardor had cooled. And right now all he had to hand were goats.

He'd read about people who felt a deep sense of peace and solemnity when milking animals. Thomas Hardy's Tess at the idyllic dairy farm in the west of England conjured up both the satisfaction of productive rural life and the aura of innocent romance as the heroine and Angel Clare are drawn together in a physical relationship. Oscar's thoughts wandered to a possible ride in the fields with Diana, surely a less simple figure than that Victorian heroine.

He knew something about genuine agricultural life, having visited the land his mother grew up on in central Missouri. It had been sold to a cousin after his grandparents found they didn't have the strength to manage the two hundred acres. While he appreciated the effort to produce food for a nation, he had little desire to engage in the labor that had exhausted his mother's parents.

A decade ago Oscar's father had built two houses side-by-side in Jefferson City, one for his own family and one for his in-laws, partly to encourage the Bahrs to move before their health failed them. The houses, neat shotgun structures, perched on a ridge a mile away south of the city's main street, their backs high above ground though the fronts were at street level.

Carl had taken on the two-house project before hard times came. After WWI and his move to Missouri, his business had grown and his reputation spread. Indeed, at one point he was a prosperous and distinguished man in the community. Oscar's early childhood was in many ways idyllic, especially as he later came to contrast it with his nomadic life in Kansas.

It had been three years since they'd been able to visit Sallie's family, though, and his mother was anxious to see her relatives. She was convinced the letters she received, mostly written by Oscar's Aunt Agnes, were hiding bad news.

When they were washing up at the spigot outside the house, Bob asked him, "You going into your dad's business, building homes, carpentry?"

"No. They want me to be a professional-- someone who doesn't get his hands dirty."

"My dad wants me to work for him in his insurance business."

"Things can change. You don't know what you have in you."

Bob sighed, "That's what you say because you're so smart."

Oscar wasn't giving his full attention to his friend's worries. Instead, he was puzzling over the odd sensation he'd felt when Bashful, trying to steel the button on his pocket, nipped him on his rear end.

Chapter Eight: The Touch

At home at night, Oscar recalled holding Diana's foot at Hedd's, her firm, shapely calf rising toward the knee, the location of the rest of her expensive stockings. Then he imagined himself and this beauty on a gently rocking farm wagon.

Picturing the conclusion to such hay-ride activity in a more private location, though, was challenging. If the hand of Babs McCauley had done anything to move Oscar along the path of understanding, it had inspired him to consider married couples--like his quiet, steady father and his intense, ambitious mother--in a new light. Other versions of his parents had to exist. But he could not conceptualize the parents he knew engaging in the operation that resulted in his birth.

Equally puzzling, those unrecognized versions of his parents were a model for himself and someone in the future. He could assume what those other people did was as carefully hidden from him now as his own late night arousals and their satisfactions were kept secret (he hoped!) from them. But it was easier to picture Tank and Diana than himself and any girl rolling around in the hay out under the cover of darkness.

During his next Saturday at work, he learned that his rival was, in fact, the one who was going to a hayride with the girl on whose feet he'd put elegant shoes. One of the three visitors who came into Hedd's that day gave Oscar the news.

"Yep," Bob told him while pretending to need shoe polish. "She was using you, like I predicted. She wanted Tank to be jealous and come crawling."

Oscar understood the logic in this. Tank, after all, had been a star athlete since seventh grade. And Oscar was an unknown newcomer. This had always been a problem coming to a new town and a new school. At college, Oscar knew, he would arrive with all the other first-year students and finally be on an equal footing in academic and romantic competition.

"Well, there are other girls," he told Bob. "Have you asked anyone?"

"No. At least not yet." His friend ran his finger over the selection of polishes. "You know, sometimes I wish I had a sister. She could find out who would be good to ask, who would appreciate going out with you."

Such an idea had never occurred to Oscar. He considered himself the lone wolf capable of finding his prey without assistance. He could easily convince himself he hadn't wanted Diana in the first place, but that still left the question of who his date should be.

Looking over his friend's shoulder, he saw Mr. Hedd outside the store. He whispered, "Here comes the boss. Better get moving." Then, as the storeowner swung open the door, he added in a louder voice, "Sorry. Tell your father we don't carry Erdal in this store."

Betty stepped in front of Mr. Hedd and asked if he would come see that she had dusted the boxes in the ladies section to his satisfaction. Bob had dropped in to gossip enough times that she knew Mr. Hedd would be irritated, so she was doing the boys a favor by distracting him. The storeowner naturally expected all his employees to be busy constantly.

Oscar believed the insistence that he and Betty be doing something every minute on the job contradicted the storeowner's larger business philosophy. "You don't make sales with goods or store furnishings, my young friend," Mr. Hedd had told him often enough. "You sell by the words you use."

"Ah," Oscar would respond every time, his eyes widening as if this were a revelation about more than getting rich.

"Every customer comes into this store wanting to hear a certain word, a word that names who he believes he is."

"So, if I say 'fireman' to Mr. Timmons, he'll walk out in new shoes?"

"You make fun, but it's the truth. Of course, you have to be more subtle than 'fireman.' See, that's what he is to the world, his profession, but not what he believes in his heart he is. For him, the word is 'aspen.'"

"'As . . . pen'?"

"Again, you laugh. Mr. Timmons grew up in Santa Fe, and his fondest memories are of hiking up into the mountains every fall with his father. Aspen leaves are golden then, and shimmer in the wind. He hears the word, and he sees the forest. You've got to touch their hearts."

"And seeing the trees, he buys shoes?"

Mr. Hedd looked out the store window, as if he were visualizing a scene from the past that was the key to his own dreams. "I can't give you the fancy philosophical or psychological reasons behind it all, my boy; but it's why I'm still in business and all the other shoe stores that were here when I started--they're gone and forgotten."

Oscar didn't have to work hard to learn the secret theme of the day's second visitor, his mother. She had come to town to buy thread--or at least that was what she had told Carl. Oscar knew she believed Mr. Hedd would not be in; and thus she could use the opportunity to remind her son of his many responsibilities, here and at home. Well, she would also make sure there were no girls distracting him.

Before she could tick off her list of reminders, however, Mr. Hedd emerged from his office. He had been doing, he explained, some end-of-the-month tabulations but was happy to see a regular customer. Sallie revealed only a part of the truth,

"I stopped by to check up on my son. I wanted to see he was doing everything he was supposed to with . . . with his arm in a sling."

"Thank you, my dear, but it's not to worry. These kids know I have my ways of finding out how they pass the time here." He looked sternly out across the store.

"Hi, Mrs. Lindbloom," said Betty, again ready to lighten the mood. "While you're here, could I show you some new pumps?"

"No, dear. This isn't a time to be buying anything. We all must be frugal, especially parents who hope to send their son to college one day."

"Now, now, Mrs. Lindbloom," Mr. Hedd insisted, "both you and your husband work hard enough, I know. You should at least take a look around. There might be something you want to put on layaway. Christmas isn't that far away." Oscar smiled to himself, as now she would have to spend at least a few minutes pretending to shop.

While Mr. Hedd was pointing out the latest inexpensive but reliable brands, Oscar whispered to Betty, "Thanks for stepping in there. I feel like there are spies on the lookout everywhere, all wanting to find me derelict in my duty.

"Oh, they just . . . they care about you, is all. But we . . . they know you always do what is right."

"Don't be too sure," Oscar grinned. "Sometimes I like to . . . experiment, find out if what other people say is really true. Have you ever smoked a pipe, for instance?"

"Oh, goodness, no! I wouldn't even want to try a cigarette."

"I bet you've had a glass of champagne sometime, though, haven't you? At a wedding?"

"All my family are teetotalers. It's the devil's brew, and you should be careful, Oscar. There are . . . there are boys around here who've gotten into trouble with drink."

She made this last statement with a look of such alarm that Oscar pulled back in surprise. Betty's eyes were wide, and it seemed as if she wanted to say more but couldn't form the words. Then he heard a much deeper voice behind him.

"Hello, Squarehead. Let me see some of your boots."

Spinning around, Oscar saw Tank, bigger, it seemed, than ever. And it looked as if he might want to chew some boots rather than wear them. Oscar would have liked to say what Gary Cooper tells Trampas in *The Virginian*: "If you wanna' call me that, smile." But he was aware that Mr. Hedd was watching from the ladies section, so he asked politely, "What size?"

"Now, that depends on where I'm going to put one of them, doesn't it." Again the grin. "Say, little girl, I think Mr. Hedd wants you to help out

62

this boy's mother." He waved a giant paw. Oscar wondered what word would unlock Tank's desire to buy--pulverize?

Betty hesitated, but Oscar assured her. "Go on, Betty. The customer is always right."

Oscar escorted Tank to a shelf on the wall where boots were displayed. "Yeah," Tank said, "And I guess you know I'm not really here to buy boots."

Oscar nodded. "I understand. You need new bedroom slippers?"

"Mr. Smart Guy," Tank said softly and leaned closer. "You're going to need crutches if you get in my way again. I'll be ready the next time you try that sucker punch."

Oscar looked over the finger Tank was wagging in his face. "Next time, Quasimodo, I won't take anything off it."

Chapter Nine: Reaching

Oscar realized he had missed an opportunity to back away from a second confrontation with Tank; but his instinctive competitiveness made him escalate rather than defuse the situation. During the next week, he hoped he hadn't made a mistake. Then, what his father told him gave him even greater pause.

"That Thompson boy," Carl said while he and Oscar were waxing the family car, a 1932 Ford V-8. "He's a pretty good football player, I hear."

"Yeah. He wrestles for school, too. He's big."

"Hmm. Up here. There is a spot." Carl pointed to the roof, which was easier for him to see because he was still several inches taller than his son. He was spreading wax which, after it dried, Oscar wiped off with a clean rag. The compound picked up dirt and left a shine. Carl paused a moment and added, "We didn't play games back in my country. It was cold, and we all had chores."

"I thought I might try to play baseball next year. Since we've moved so much, I've never had the chance to compete."

"It has been hard, I know. But you've had food on the table. Your mother . . . she misses her home, maybe more than I miss mine."

Oscar stood on his toes to reach the middle of the roof. He saw his father rubbing wax onto the hood, his injured right hand still exerting more force that Oscar's young arm could. "Did you . . . did you hear that I had a bit of run-in with Tank . . . with Mark Thompson . . . at the fair."

"Yah, I did. One of the men at work, he told me. He said you handled him right well, but I'll tell you something, boy: you be careful now. Don't pick a fight with him just to show you're better. There are other ways to beat out a rival."

Oscar studied his father's face, impenetrable as always. Carl worked out in the sun so much that his skin was dark and lined. While there were occasions when he would smile, he did not laugh. If he was upset, Oscar had learned, his father would rub his forehead, bringing his fingers down across his eyes. But he seldom expressed his feelings.

"I didn't start anything with him the other time, but I don't want to back down. He was insulting the girl I was with." Oscar knew this wasn't quite accurate, as the insults had been directed at him. And now Tank was taking that same girl to the hayride.

Carl stood up straight and rubbed his hands on the old piece of towel he had been using. "The men at work, they say that Tank is not stupid. He's big and strong, but he's also smart. So, I say to you again, watch how you go with that boy."

This was about as lengthy a speech as Carl would ever utter, especially one giving Oscar advice. His method of raising a son had always been to set the example and assume his intelligent boy would understand what he was to do and what not to do.

Oscar paused in his work, too. "I understand, Dad. I'll be careful."

Moving to the part of the hood where the wax was dry, he resumed wiping. Now and then he caught sight of the thumb on his father's right hand; it ended at the knuckle. A year after he purchased his first table saw, a few days before Oscar was born, Carl had pushed a board through the blade and through that one digit. It happened in a flash. All he said, according to Oscar's mother, was, "Yee, whiz." He wrapped the thumb tip in a rag and walked to the doctor's office, but there was nothing to be done in those days.

He could still perform almost any task with that hand, but there were times when his grip was less strong and his ability to maneuver restricted. Oscar could not understand how the man who, as far as he knew, never made a mistake had cut off a portion of his thumb.

Oscar believed his own broken wrist was only a temporary handicap. The doctor had shortened the cast, and the rest might be taken off before the hayride. He hoped that was the case because he was determined to attend. He didn't want Tank or Diana to feel they had kept him from the event, though he was still wondering who his date should be.

For years afterwards Oscar believed he ended up inviting Betty Devine to the hayride out of pity. And there was some truth to that idea, as she was an attractive girl and it was a shame that no one had asked her. It certainly hadn't been Oscar's intention that Saturday before homecoming, but Ernest Hemingway's voice got into his head and shaped his future.

Oscar had finished The *Sun Also Rises* the night before, having read the whole book in just a few days. Walking to work the next morning, he knew the conversations he was carrying on in his head--with his father, with Bob, with Tank--were infected by Hemingway's terse prose style and the novel's soulless ennui.

He had adopted the styles of other favorite authors before, though he too often figured out what he should have said in the manner of an Edgar Rice Burroughs' hero only after the event. And sometimes the desire to sound like the jaded Count Vronsky led to his saying something he regretted.

Still, Oscar didn't understand why the figure of Robert Cohn from *The Sun Also Rises* was also haunting him. Cohn is a foil for Hemingway's hero and narrator, Jake Barnes. In the first chapter Jake acknowledges his companion's ability (middleweight champion at Princeton) but belittles his success by saying it was merely an effort to overcome shyness.

Oscar admired the contrasting stoic toughness of Jake, impotent from an unspecified war injury but still the man for the book's heroine, Brett Ashley. Part of Oscar, though, also wanted to be someone who can methodically dispose of multiple antagonists the way Cohn does.

During a slow time at Hedd's, he said to Betty, "It's cool at night now. Cold for a hayride under a gray sky."

"Oh, you're going?" Betty was unpacking a case of inserts for women's shoes.

"Hmm? Ah, well, there's nothing else to do. But what does it matter, anyway?" He studied the green sales tickets speared on a spike beside the cash register. Some were several weeks old, but Mr. Hedd thought a full stack made customers believe the store was busy.

"Oh, it doesn't mean much to boys, of course. But for some girls . . . "

"Yeah, sad ones. They think it's how they'll find the boy of their dreams." He gazed toward the street, as if it and all roads led nowhere.

Betty had organized the inserts in rough categories: those designed to stop odor; those that provided support; those that cushion against rubbing. "I'd kind of like to go myself, maybe, but my parents are . . . they worry about what happens on these outings, even though they're very well chaperoned."

Oscar sighed. "Nothing happens, good or bad. Teachers and parents all around . . . why do they bother?" He would have liked to pull out a cigarette and cup it against the wind, as if it would be his last. "Anyway, you go if you want to."

"You're right, of course. But a girl . . . well, she has to be asked. And . . . . " Scooping up a handful of inserts designed to absorb oder, she hurried over to the display shelf.

Oscar thought again of Robert Cohn, whose skill as a boxer is repeatedly contrasted with his social ineptitude, partly deriving from the fact that he is Jewish. He has the ability to floor Jake and even the champion bullfighter, Romero. On the other hand, Cohn, confused in his rejection by women, is often crying as he's fighting. Oscar will make simple statements, no blubbering.

Today, Betty was the one crying. Oscar saw her stopped in the middle of arranging the inserts and staring into space. A line of tears came from each eye.

"What the hell," Oscar said to himself. He left the cash register and walked over to her, "I'll take you. Your mom likes me, and she'll approve."

"You're . . . you're asking me to the hayride?"

"Yeah. You should go." He thought to himself, "I've might as well go with her as with anyone. Poor girl, she needs a break."

"Oh, Oscar, that's so nice!" she beamed. "We'll have such a wonderful time. You'll see."

Did he actually say to her, "Yes, isn't it pretty to think so"? Even the next day, he couldn't remember if he just thought the words or said them out loud.. He hoped he hadn't, but he couldn't be sure. "Poor bastard," he called himself.

In the end, of course, Betty was right. He had a wonderful time.

Chapter Ten: Hugs

Even though the night was arriving earlier now and a cover of clouds darkened the sky, Oscar had slipped out of his dark existentialist mood and was pleased at the prospect of taking part in a school activity. It's true that he wouldn't have the girl on his arm other boys wanted, but nobody disliked his date. And he would feel one of the group.

As the evening went on, Oscar enjoyed playing the role of courteous gentleman: bending a knee to help Betty up on the wagon, offering his jacket if she were cold, making it clear that he was pleased to be her escort. He accepted graciously the shy, quick, chaste hug she gave him when they said good night at the school.

He also felt he had been generous to his friend. When Bob announced that he was going stag on the hayride, Oscar invited him to sit with him and Betty. "Just don't bring Sleepy or Bashful," he had teased. "They would eat all the hay . . . and our pants . . . and the wagons."

"Mrs. Aire told me there are quite a few 'singles' coming," Bob said defensively. "She said everyone should enjoy things like this, especially now, when no one can tell what the future holds."

Oscar knew people were increasingly concerned about possible war in Europe. Mr. Hedd, Mr. Lewis, and others were arguing we shouldn't ignore what Hitler was doing. But when he watched Errol Flynn in *The Charge of the Light Brigade,* Oscar, like most Americans, concluded all wars occurred on distant landscapes like Asia and in the past of previous centuries.

He could perhaps fantasize himself saving his brother (if he had one), even if they were rivals for the love of the same woman; but he would never find himself in a situation to do so. And, in daydreams inspired by the movie, Oscar, miraculously survived the suicidal assault at Balaklava to win the beautiful Olivia de Havilland.

But any conflict "over there," he continued to believe, wasn't going to affect this country in general or him in particular. By this time next year he would be a college freshman at a prestigious university. So, even if the country went to war, he was confident no one would want to turn his potential as a scientist or musician or writer into cannon fodder.

As he would learn, however, a war might be fought overseas and its effects invade America. The woman to whom he would propose marriage one day would be scarred by war before she met him.

Another error in his predicting also derived from false notions of his ability to function as free agent, a trait he shared with many in his generations, especially Midwesterners and

Westerners. When he left home, he naively believed he would be completely independent.

Oscar hadn't told his parents about his plans to go on to college a year early, though he knew he would have to have that talk with them soon. He didn't anticipate serious objections. After all, his father had not only left home to work in the coal mines when he was younger than Oscar was now, but he'd also emigrated from his country with two brothers to start a new life in a different country. Carl would probably be proud of his son's initiative.

His mother had married an immigrant and eventually left her family, moving to Kansas. Though he anticipated she might oppose his decision initially, she could be persuaded--or so he believed. However, her grip on his future was stronger than he knew. While he was winning physical battles with boys his age, the emotional struggle with his mother would not produce the clear victory he thought he had won after he broke his wrist the second time.

Oscar did understand that his parents believed in his ultimate success, even if they repeatedly stressed that the road there would be long and arduous. They scoffed, for instance, at the popular new game, Monopoly, and almost forbid him to play because it fostered a conviction that you could gain great riches by the throw of a dice. Still, he and Bob enjoyed marathon sessions at the Peterson home.

Confident that he was continuing his rise to prominence at Salinas High School and preparing to own one day such properties as Park Place and Boardwalk, Oscar rode comfortably along with Betty over the Prescotts' farm. Their backs against a single hay bale, he observed, "It must have been lonely out here when the first settlers arrived. Those were difficult times."

In his mind he was mixing what he saw around him with scenes from Edna Ferber's *Cimarron*. That novel about the Oklahoma land rush featured a couple moving from Wichita, Kansas, to "Osage" Oklahoma. And, looking out at the open landscape, indirectly lit by lights around the house and barn, Oscar imagined himself singlehandedly settling the West.

"These are difficult times, too, Oscar. I'm so glad to know . . . to know that others care about me." He suspected she wanted to say Jesus cared for her, and for him. He did not want to dismiss her beliefs; but, if he could, he would channel the conversation elsewhere.

"Our pioneer forefathers were pretty much on their own our here. Nature can be a cruel host, you know, and only the toughest survive."

While Ferber's central character, Yancy Gravat, was inspired by a flamboyant Texas lawyer--also a skilled gunfighter--the novel recounted his establishing a newspaper, the *Oklahoma Wigwam*, and carving out a life against powerful competing groups in chaotic times.

Oscar liked his ability to stand up to others as well as his intellectual strength.

"My parents are blessed. Father's work at the mill has been steady." He was the bookkeeper. "And Mother is a wonderful gardener. We put up so many beans and so much corn this year, we'll have plenty all winter."

"She's the ant, not the grasshopper."

"The ant . . . ?"

"In Aesop's fable. The grasshopper didn't plan for winter, spending all his time singing and enjoying life. The ant worked hard to put away the food they would need."

"Ah. Well," she giggled, "I think you and I must be benefiting from all our hard work at Hedd's." He laughed as well. Such shared pleasant experiences, however, were not what he was to remember years after this event. He would be haunted by the fact that he had been ambushed before the hayride began.

After the homecoming parade Oscar was to meet Betty at the school, where a bus would take everyone to the farm. As he approached E. Republic Street, Oscar was woolgathering about his future one minute and then found himself lifted off his feet in another.

Giant arms had wrapped around his chest, and his breath was expelled in a violent rush. He was spun around in a circle, and he prepared to be thrown to the ground. It was as if Tarzan had been caught off guard by Terkoz and had no knife to match his foe's sharp fangs.

Behind him he heard a grunt that he knew came from the man-mountain he had called Quasimodo. And the hot air in his ear was the breath of his arch enemy, ready to exact revenge for being floored at the county fair. Tank had him in a bear hug and Oscar was sure he would now be . . . well, pulverized.

Then he heard another sound, the clatter of a car engine and the grinding of tires on pavement. What was that?

"You okay, Squarehead?" asked his assailant. And Oscar discovered he had been let go.

He spun around and assumed a boxer's stance, despite the fact that his arm had not been free of its cast for a full day. But why had Tank given up the advantage of his bear hug?

Then, out of the corner of his eye, he saw a Ford Model A lumbering down the street.

"You need to look where you're going, four-eyes," laughed Tank. "Your head was in the clouds, and you're damn lucky I happened to spot you stepping into traffic."

"I . . . I . . . " Oscar looked again at the automobile chugging steadily away, then on all sides to see if he and Tank had had an audience. He did: Diana, dressed in a style more elegant than necessary for a hayride, was watching with a thinly suppressed smile.

"I think what you want to say is 'T'anks, Tank' but I can read it in your eyes."

Oscar did say it, but more as a question. "Thanks?"

Of course, he was beginning to understand: Salinas' version of Clay Center's Old Man McCort had been cruising down E. Republic, some old codger everyone knew to avoid. Lost in dreams, Oscar had been as oblivious to his surroundings as this driver had been to pedestrians.

Tank, glancing first this way, then that, leaned close and jabbed a monstrous forefinger in Oscar's chest. "You know, Squarehead. That was a lot more fun than beating the Scandinavian out of you." He threw back his head and laughed. "And now, you owe me."

Oscar knew he did. For all his ability to create fantastic scenarios, though, he could never imagine the way in which he would be able repay his debt--with urine. In the meantime, he vowed, he would try much harder to keep his feet on the ground.

Book Two: Hands On.
Chapter Eleven: Tuning

"I can play this thing," Professor Lewis told Oscar gesturing at his piano, "but I'll be darned if I know how it works."

He was leaning over the cabinet, the lid propped as high as it would go. He stared at the action. Hammers, hammer shanks, hammer flange, main action rail, and action bracket were on top; beneath them and partially visible were the backcheck, the repetition levers, the hammer knuckles, the wippen, the letoff rail, and the wippen rail.

"It sounded good as I came down the hall. Is it not doing right?" Oscar asked, looking over his shoulder.

Professor Lewis sighed. "There are some notes in the upper register that just don't ring true. It's not quite the pitch but the sound. Something in the innards has gone out of whack." He waved a useless hand at what he saw.

"Could we use one of the other pianos for my session this one time?"

Oscar knew his teacher wouldn't like that. The practice pianos were old uprights constantly going out of tune with the banging of beginning students. Plus, this was Professor Lewis' own baby grand, placed at the expense of the usual faculty office furniture. He liked to have his lessons here; and, late in the day and sometimes into evening, he would to play for himself. It became his own private world.

Oscar added, "I could come back tomorrow and take a look."

"You can repair a piano?"

"My father has replaced some of the pieces, and I've studied the works. It's fascinating--all the connected wood and wire parts, the systems of sound, amplification, dampening."

Oscar learned how the instrument works--the force of the depressed key transmitted through four connected pieces making the felt-covered hammer strike the string--from a detailed encyclopedia article. He knew there were dampening mechanisms, repetition structures, the front rail, front key pin, front rail punching.

In a college textbook he had explored the underlying physics of machines: the mechanics of levers and pulleys, the action and reaction of colliding objects, the principles of momentum and inertia; wave oscillation, interference, resonance. If asked, he could have diagrammed the piano's workings with vectors and formula.

"I'd get Jackson to look at this immediately," said Professor Lewis. "But he's out . . . with the flu. So, could you drop by after school? I have a new, gifted student coming in tomorrow."

Jackson, called at his time a "Negro," had no first name so far as Oscar knew. He kept all the music department's instruments in tune and functioning. He could play any of them by ear and had his own combo appearing Friday nights at the Salinas Hi-Hat. Some locals claimed he was as good as more famous musicians (like Count Basie) heard in the Kansas City clubs.

"I have an hour between my last class and my job. I promise not to break anything--just see if I can spot an obvious flaw."

"Hmm. Well, okay. Meanwhile you need to show me how you're coming with that Bach I gave you. After all, it's your last lesson of the year, and that cast's off been been off for weeks."

Oscar flinched, as he had gradually come to realize he would never recover full flexibility in that hand. The break had been set awkwardly for the second time, and he couldn't hide the fact much longer from himself, his teacher, or--perhaps most worrisome--his mother.

Part of him was depressed at this realization because he knew he had talent and loved music. He also valued his relationship with Professor Lewis, who, he had learned, was troubled by more than the odd sound of his piano. His teacher was alarmed at German troops in the Rhineland and the undercurrent he had felt in news reports of the Summer Olympics.

Oscar understood that Professor Lewis' spirits were brightened when his students did well; so he practiced hard to keep his teacher's attention on the local rather than the global.

On the other hand, the thought that he would not become a piano virtuoso had been liberating for Oscar. He'd picked up the instrument of another Kansas City musician, Charlie Parker, and was feeling that the saxophone might be his proper medium of expression. And he wondered if jazz, not classical music, could be the language of his soul.

He still wanted to continue studying music theory, the grand schemes of harmony, rhythm, and timing--all of which are more accessible through keyboard instruments than woodwinds. What Professor Lewis called the Mystical Froth of Fifths captured his instinct for the ideal. It is often represented (if inaccurately, according to his teacher) by a circle.

The music faculty at Salinas Wesleyan, like most in the profession, believed that the geometric figure of a circle could represent the universe of harmonic possibilities. Placing the key of C (no sharps) at twelve o'clock, one could advance to the right around the circle through all the keys, raising the tonic a fifth and adding a sharp for each hour. Moving counterclockwise by descending fifths, each key adds a flat. Starting at any pitch and ascending by a fifth, one passes all twelve tones in an octave clockwise, returning to the beginning pitch.

Professor Lewis, who had studied Eastern music more than his colleagues, frequently pointed to anomalies in this representation and to alternative theories about natural sounds and the conditioning of social constructs. "Froth," he insisted, was an apt term for the idea.

The totality of the generally accepted system, though, was appealing to Oscar. And he linked it to the medieval concept of the music of the spheres, each heavenly body in its crystalline sphere emitting a note, the whole sounding the harmony of God's creation. From the earth upward hover the moon, sun, planets, fixed stars--all moved by the primum mobile.

Oscar thrilled to those classic works that represented such unity, as when Milton's Adam, still in the Garden of Eden, instructs Eve about the perfection of God's universe, urging her to hear "Celestial voices to the midnight air, / Sole, or responsive each to others note / Singing thir great Creator . . ." Even the music played in the present sometimes seemed to reach toward such perfection.

Of course, if such systems were connected to contemporary religion, Oscar adopted the attitude of another of his favorite literary characters, Mark Twain's Huck Finn. After that rebellious boy is instructed by the Widow Douglas' sister "'about the good place [where] all a body would have to do there was to go around all day long with a harp and sing, forever and ever,'" Huck "didn't think much of it." And neither did Oscar.

Experimenting with Catherine Roger's instrument one day after band practice, though, he did feel another sense of aesthetic satisfaction-- the appeal of a single, sweet line of melody. Well, and an appreciation of one girl's beauty.

Cathy had been complaining, "I just can't make my fingers do what they're supposed to! They're not long enough or strong enough. I think I should be playing the piccolo!" Oscar hadn't paid any attention to her fingers, though they were famous for creating elaborate string figures. Her long legs and shapely behind dominated his understanding of her physical being.

"Let me see," he said and reached out for the horn.

Even his awkward attempt to play the beginning of 'Cake Walkin' Babies from Home" made him feel he could move through varied expressions of a powerful theme to completed expression. And the hand position didn't put undue pressure on his left wrist, perhaps because the sling around his neck bore the weight.

Cathy played well herself, though Oscar and others wondered if she shouldn't switch from the tenor to alto sax, given her diminutive--if highly attractive--form. But she liked the deeper tone of the larger horn and could carry it while marching in parades as well as the boys.

Cathy's strength, agility, and coordination, along with her compact body, made her the ideal cheerleader. And her cartwheeling figure was the image many Salinas boys chased across their dreams that year, especially after it was explained that Catholic girls would let boys explore more than others because they could just confess later and be absolved of sin.

Oscar fantasized about Catherine as much as anyone. His mental musings fluctuated that fall between arrangements of an octave's twelve notes (whole plus half tones) and the coordinated jitter bug steps Cathy and her friends could sometimes energetically pursue after band practice.

One of his secret goals for the family trip to Missouri early in the new year was to find something saxophone-related to bring back for Cathy. He would say the idea came to him because she was letting him borrow her horn from time to time, but he really wanted to see if she was interested in having a partner in more than musical exploration. He found she would be.

Chapter Twelve: Drops

Oscar had been recruited into the school band to play the timpani and the xylophone. The new director, a friend of Professor Lewis, knew Oscar could read music and quickly determined that he had the necessary dexterity to execute the rolls. Oscar was willing because he saw it as another opportunity to pursue romance. After all, where else but in a band should he look for someone with whom he might make beautiful music? And he quickly spotted Catherine.

Too, his friend, Bob, a competent tuba player, had encouraged him. "The timpani are great. No need to tune, clean and clear, fantastic in all the big numbers--Bach's *Tönet, ihr Pauken!*, the scherzo of Beethoven's *Ninth*, Berlioz with *Symphonie Fantastique*."

"We're going to play those!"

"Nah. I'm just giving you an idea of what we might perform, especially with the new director, Mrs. Balogh. She's European and really a professional."

"Hmm. Well, you know I'm ready for challenges."

"All you have to do for parades and football games is bang the xylophone with a hammer."

"True, though I may get more than a few knocks myself from the likes of Tank."

"Shoot, his crowd will mock anyone who plays a musical instrument. Might as well have fun. The spring band trip is great, especially when we're coming back by bus in the dark."

Every year Salinas High School took part in a state-wide competition in Lawrence. The band entered in two categories, concert and marching, raising the money in a number of events through the winter. One major program was a concert in the town hall, for which they usually sold several hundred tickets. One reason Mrs. Balogh had looked for a timpani player was so they could perform an as yet unpublished piece by a fellow Hungarian composer in February.

This attractive, mature woman had come to town the previous spring, married but without her husband. Rumor circulated that he could not leave his homeland, though no one knew exactly why.

The boys noticed her quickly when school started up as, despite her conservative dress and quiet demeanor, she possessed a subtle beauty. And, when she conducted, she became another woman--fiery-eyed, dynamic, intense.

Bob told Oscar, "And with Mrs. Balogh this year, the band trip will be even more exciting. She's . . . she's . . . "

Oscar understood his friend's enthusiasm about this teacher: he felt Bob was drawn to older women. He was shy around girls his age, but with women five or ten years older, who had the social skills to direct conversation, he opened up. Mrs. Balogh was perhaps in her mid thirties.

"Bob," Oscar teased, "I do have to ask you: does she like goats?"

He grunted. "Not as much as Diana Light does."

He was referring to the rampant rumors that she and Tank (the animal) were enjoying more than each other's company. Oscar had already decided to put his competition for that beauty behind him. She had flirted with him, he concluded--just as Bob had predicted--to incite Tank's jealousy, not to win her heart . . . or other body parts. And now there was Cathy.

There was Cathy, though a part of that saxophone-playing wonder did bother Oscar: the spit.

When he first asked to try her instrument, Catherine had said, "Here, you use this old reed." And that made sense: he had to put his lips on the mouthpiece, which she'd just had between hers. (Of course, he did hope their mouths might come together at some point, but not around the same thin sliver of wood.)

"I'll give it back," he assured her.

She answered in a way that Oscar was pleased to interpret as an invitation. "If you're going to do this more than once, you could get your own reed at Shangri-La." That was the one music store in Salinas.

"I might just do that," he said smiling. In the back of his mind he heard Charlie Parker playing "My Old Flame" and imagined himself echoing that evocative portrait of women with "fascinating ways / A fascinating gaze in their eyes." Cathy's gaze would be fascinated at his quick mastery of her own instrument.

But, when he got ready to take the sax from Cathy, he was shocked to see a puddle between her feet. "What's that?" he asked, almost as if he worried that she'd had the kind of accident a first grader might.

"Saliva." She laughed. "You didn't know woodwinds are spit-producing factories?"

He'd seen--but not really paid attention to--all the woodwind players swabbing their instruments after practice. He'd assumed that this was some sort of polishing procedure, perhaps eliminating anything that might detract from a pure sound. He'd also noticed that the trumpet and trombone players would frequently push a button on their horns and blow, bringing forth only a hiss, and then shake them vigorously. It hadn't occur to him that saliva condenses in the horn when it's played, tiny droplets carried in warm breath collecting on the cooler insides of the instrument. It pools at the horn's low points, the bottom, for instance, of the sax's J shape. Oscar recalled the illustration that had accompanied an encyclopedia article on hydraulics--of course!

"Well, Mr. Scientist, the human body is 99% water, so that's just a tiny part of me."

Oscar wasn't about to correct Cathy (he knew her H_2O was less than that), but he did decide, if he were going to play a saxophone regularly, he would get a reed of his own. In his head, he heard sadly, "My new lovers all seem so tame / For I haven't met a gal / So innocent or elegant / As my old flame."

Later, he was surprised to find his father approved of his experimentation with instruments other than the piano. "You have a great uncle--well now, he was my great uncle . . . but anyway, he played for the King. You come from a family of musicians."

"I didn't know that. What did he play?"

"The clarinet. I didn't know him, but cousins told me about his performing at the court and in orchestras across Sweden. So, you should see what you can do with that horn there." He gestured at the golden instrument hanging in the sling around Oscar's neck. Oscar noted his father's rough hands, the dirt from cleaning and oiling of tools.

Oscar had taken Catherine's saxophone home at the end of school on a Friday, to try it for a day; but he was playing in the garage where it was less likely his mother would hear. Carl had a workbench and tools in a small room off the garage and heard the beginners' starts and stops.

"I'm really in the band to play the timpani, but I like this sound. It can be like a person singing." He meant like a woman, a woman with a deep, throaty voice, a woman in love.

"You'll still be working on the piano, though," said Carl, an assertion, not a question. "Your mother, she counts on your doing well."

Oscar had not been able to fix the problem with his teacher's piano, but he did spot two tiny hairline fractures in neighboring hammer shanks. Jackson had replaced them the next day.

"Professor Lewis does want me to remain as his student, though not after I graduate. He thinks I should go on to a better university." Oscar was already envisioned himself at center stage, though now not at a college concert hall. Instead, he saw himself in front of a microphone in a major radio studio, behind him a small combo--bass, drums, piano.

His father studied him, rubbing his forehead and bringing his fingers down across his eyes. "Well, now, that's more than a year away. And times, they are still hard. We have to find ways to pay for your schooling."

Oscar began to break the saxophone into its parts in order to fit it back in the case. "One idea I had . . . maybe it would be good for me to begin college next year. That way I could start earning a living myself earlier, and that would help . . . " He ran the swab on a string Cathy had given him through the horn's body and wiped the mouthpiece thoroughly with a towel.

His father watched him slide the reed into a cardboard holder and clean the keys. "You're doing your share now at the shoe store. And you can continue that while you're at Wesleyan." He said this in such a way that there was no possibility for disagreement. "Your mother . . . she wouldn't take it well if you wanted to go to school in another place."

"But if I could get a scholarship, and the chance to really succeed was there . . . ?"

Carl glanced toward the house. "I will tell you something, son. I had to go away from home to work when I was younger than you are. And my mother, she was already gone. You don't want to leave your family, I will say that to you."

It was a long time before Oscar realized that Carl was also referring to himself here, that he did not want his son to leave him. As Oscar came to understand with some pain, his father knew it would be very hard on him if Sallie didn't have Oscar to brighten her days.

Chapter Thirteen: Kubb

If Oscar's father had been able to tell his son at that moment some of the things he had experienced in his marriage--the years before Sallie became pregnant--the crisis of that winter might have been avoided. But Carl, like so many Scandinavians, kept his feelings to himself and believed that husband and wife had to protect their children from adult problems.

There had been more than economic factors leading to his decision to work in Kansas rather than Missouri. But Oscar would only learn this when he arrived--out of work and down to a borrowed fifteen dollars--at his Aunt Agnes' after his graduation from college.

As proficient as he was in his school work, Oscar didn't use his analytical abilities to see beneath the surface of his parents' home life. He had realized his mother consistently found reasons not to accompany her husband on Sunday trips out to the Swedish community in Assyria. But he accepted at face value her claims that she needed to rest from her usual chores on the Lord's day, that she would use the time to write letters home, that the weather was uncertain.

Sallie had to accept Carl's visiting his relatives south of Salinas because several opportunities for employment had resulted. The

Lindbloom men, though fiercely independent, could get more contracts working together. And Lars and Nils had been in this area for years.

Carl had lived here, too, of course, when he first arrived in the country; but after the First World War he had become so successful that he could move to a part of the country that resembled his native land. And in Missouri he'd met Sallie.

When the Depression began, his work in and around Jefferson City dried up, and Carl's savings continued to shrink. So, he took on odd jobs in Emporia, Kansas, then Herrington, and finally Clay Center until he realized he needed the support of family. A single life insurance policy he had carried since his wedding represented the last of his reserves.

The Lindbloom brothers' favorite job was house building, but they would restore any building or take on repair work when necessary. Carl, the most skilled carpenter and builder of the three, preferred to let his brothers deal with clients while he concentrated on the actual work. Lars was an exceptional paper hanger, so fast that he often had time to sit on a sawhorse and smoke his pipe as Nils struggled to get paste on the walls ahead of him. All three would paint, though Carl generally did the fine work.

When Oscar's mother said the Sunday he had taken Cathy's saxophone home with him, "I must finish this sewing for Mrs. Lewis," he didn't think anything about it. Sallie added, "You two go along when you're ready, but be home in time for dinner. I have a casserole ready for the oven." At a later date, Oscar would understand she used meals to limit Carl's time with his siblings and their families. But today he was looking forward to challenging his great uncle Gunter in kubb and didn't think about reasons behind her statement.

Back in the summer, when the family had arrived in Salinas, he'd met his uncles, aunts, and cousins as a grown boy. He'd only seen them once before, when he was too young to remember names and history. On those initial visits he worried it might be suggested he follow in the family's line of work. But this immigrant generation wanted their children to get an education and move up into the professions. None of his male cousins was trained in trades. (No woman except Aunt Kristina worked outside the home, though they put in long hours on the farms.)

Since he and his father came on Sundays, a day of rest for this Lutheran community, Oscar was not asked to help with plowing, cultivating, or harvesting. Working the mules was difficult to begin with, and they recognized unfamiliar hands on the reins. He'd also enough experience with Bob's goats to appreciate the challenge of dealing with livestock. Only when a crisis came to the farming community in the years that followed-- grasshopper plague, jackrabbits eating the beets, tornado damage--would Oscar be asked to take a role in the fields.

Through this autumn, he got to know his cousins as together they explored the little town or played games in fields. When they were inside, Oscar would hear the older family members sharing their memories of the past, worries about the future, the latest news from relatives still in Europe--often in their native language. Those sing-song, Swedish conversations were a pleasant background to his talk with relatives his own age. At times he could even imagine an Alexandra Bergson, heroine of *O, Pioneers!*, somewhere in this community.

Oscar recalled that "tall, strong girl" at the beginning of Willa Cather's novel: "she walked rapidly and resolutely, as if she knew exactly where she was going and what she was going to do next." Oscar, believing in his own importance, was convinced that a present day counterpart would only be waiting for the right young man to help her shape the future of America.

One female cousin--well, a distant cousin-- did appear to seek out Oscar. Elsa Svenson seemed starstruck by the boy who was already known to be smart and good with his fists. (When they reached ninth grade, those in Assyria who could rode into town for school.)

"I saw you this week," she said when he joined the crowd around the kubb pitch.

She had the blond beauty and athletic build for which Scandinavian women are famous, though she was still slender and girlish. Oscar felt himself far too old and mature to be interested in her.

"At Hedd's? I'm usually in the back on weekdays." He kept his attention on the battle between her father and his father. They were both good, but Carl never took the game as seriously as Gunter.

"It was down by Shangri-La. You were talking to Betty Devine out on the street."

He thought back to Wednesday, before he went to work to the storeroom. "Ah, yes. She works with me on Saturdays. We were probably talking shop." He also wondered what Elsa was doing in town after school.

"She's a pretty girl, and so nice. Do you and she . . . um . . . go places together?"

He laughed, "Oh, no. She's . . . just a friend."

Oscar's romantic life included Betty only as an audience for his tales of conquest. Despite the good time they'd had together at the homecoming hayride, he never thought of her as a prospective lover, even in the face of the more than occasional hints she offered.

Elsa said, "My father doesn't think I'm ready to see boys. Do you think I'm too young?"

"Look at that throw by your father! He's going to win again."

"Will you be coming out here for Christmas? We all have such a good time." Then, perhaps realizing that having presents for all these relatives might be a strain on Oscar's parents, she added, "Of course, mostly we sing Christmas songs, make gingerbread biscuits, wait for Tomte to hand out gifts."

"Tomte?"

"You don't know? Oh, he's a forest gnome . . . Aunt Kristina plays the part. She's hilarious with her funny rhymes. And there's the big smorgasbord." Oscar didn't want to reveal how little he knew of such Old World customs, so he nodded knowingly.

Elsa was also thinking about the rice porridge with an almond hidden it. The tradition is that the one who finds the almond will be married in the following year.

"Look, your father has won again." Carl was shaking Gunter's hand and looking around to see who would be Gunter's next opponent. Oscar stepped forward.

"So, you're going to take on the champion," said his father approvingly. "Yah, good luck, then."

The game of kubb involves throwing wooden sticks at wooden blocks. The player who knocks his opponent's king over is the winner, but other intermediate objectives have to be achieved first;

and both offensive and defensive strategy can be complicated.

Uncle Gunter was the acknowledged champion of the family, but Oscar believed he would dethrone him, once he'd had enough practice. Oscar had beaten many of his older, married cousins and had already been recognized for his accuracy in throwing. But he didn't have enough experience to understand the complexity of position.

At the center of the field is the king, but each player has ten knights that must be toppled first. When a player's knight is down, he or she throws it in the field, positioning it to block his opponent or to create a situation where he might knock the king down prematurely and thus lose.

Oscar had noticed that Gunter often fell behind early in his matches, only to stage a miraculous comeback. When he didn't understand was this was a deliberate strategy, shaping the field to his advantage.

On this day, surprisingly, Gunter failed to turn the game around at the end, and Oscar celebrated triumphantly. In the thrill of anticipated victory, he didn't see his opponent, just before making his final flawed toss, wink at his daughter.

Chapter Fourteen: Mechanics

The ride back to town was quiet. As he drove, Carl rubbed his forehead and brought his fingers down across his eyes, leading Oscar to conclude that the brothers didn't have prospects for more work. As they turned onto their street, his father did offer one observation about his family. "That Elsa, now. She is a pretty girl."

"Yes," said Oscar absentmindedly. He would take the borrowed saxophone back to the truly pretty girl (Catherine) tomorrow; and he was determined to ask her to go with him to see Greta Garbo and Robert Taylor in *Camille* the following weekend.

Oscar and his father were riding in the family's 1932 Ford V-8, a fortunate purchase Carl had made from a banker in Clay Center. The man had been pleased with the house Carl had built for him, and he offered the car, only two years old, at such a low price that it was as much a bonus as an expenditure. Oscar still felt proud to ride in the powerful automobile and was always willing to help his father wax the body and clean the interior.

When Carl first bought it home, Oscar was so interested in the mechanics that his father borrowed a shop service repair manual from a local dealer for his son. The boy was intrigued with the procedures for setting the timing, fine tuning the ignition, adjusting the carburetor, removing or repairing the clutch and differential. As if he were preparing to work on automobiles, Oscar studied the specifications for valve grinding, lubrication techniques, wiring tests. In his mind he linked the numbers in itemized lists to figures in the step-by-step, illustrated instructions. Maybe one day he would design cars for the world.

He knew it would be a long time before he had his own car, even years before he would be allowed to use this one. But, borrowing from provocative newspaper photos of the infamous Bonnie and Clyde with their 1932 Ford V-8 leaving Joplin, Missouri on Route 66, he imagined himself traveling through some some distant city, a handsome man attracting women who were fearless and sexually adventurous. He would not be an outlaw exactly, but still a man who didn't conform to all of society's expectations and rules.

As he and his father pulled into the garage, it occurred to Oscar that their Assyria relatives did not stop by to visit in town. Nils, Lars, and Pers had been on hand, along with several of their children, to help unload the rented truck when they arrived in the summer; but contact after that had occurred elsewhere. Sallie's attitude, Oscar had to admit, was probably one reason.

"I suppose we can make this work," his mother had said dismissively that first day in Salinas, scowling at the small house in a modest neighborhood southeast of the city center. Their moves in search of work had taken them from the comfortable house Carl built next door to Oscar's grandparents in Jefferson City to smaller and less well kept structures

Uncle Pers had found this house after Carl wrote they would be moving from Clay Center. Sallie preferred that her husband come ahead to take care of these matters himself, but his last job required attention right up to the day of their departure. She hoped they would soon move to a home of their own.

"It won't cost that much to keep warm," observed Oscar's father. He had studied the coal furnace in the half basement. Floor vents opened in the living room, kitchen, and bedroom. Oscar would sleep in a snug room built into the attic, heat rising through a floor register. It had two small windows, allowing him to survey the street and the backyard.

Sallie sighed as she looked for places to put kitchen utensils. "I'll need to make some bright curtains if I'm to stay in here all day." There was a tiny utility room with a large laundry sink to one side and storage shelves--almost a pantry--on the other. She did all their clothes by hand and put up fruits and vegetables when they were available.

Carl looked through the same window. "There's space for a garden here." He would break the ground for her, but raising vegetables was a woman's responsibility.

"The soil's not what it is along the Osage River." Some of her relatives still worked the same land her grandparents had cleared when they migrated from Tennessee.

Oscar tried to lift their mood. "I like my room. It's the kind of garret a poet or a composer would live in and produce a masterpiece."

In a library book he had seen Henry Wallis' famous portrait of English poet Thomas Chatterton. The teenage genius had taken poison by his own hand, and his body was draped across his bed, head hanging over the edge. It was an iconic image of the aspiring writer unrecognized by a materialistic world. When Oscar learned later that an ancestor had been an accomplished musician in Sweden, he wondered if he had inherited the tragic touch of genius.

From time to time Oscar asked his dad about their ancestors, especially as they traveled away from Missouri to different Kansas towns, always moving closer to the Lindbloom family. He'd gotten only a sketchy picture, but now he wanted to construct--at least in his head--a family tree.

Like most boys, he didn't consider his maternal ancestors as a source of his own abilities or personality. The Old World structure of patriarchy shaped his thoughts. Too, he knew his mother's people had been hunters and farmers moving west with the frontier, away from civilization. Her desire for education and a rise in social status was unusual.

Oscar's musings about family were brought into sharper focus that week when Betty asked him,"Have you done all your Christmas shopping? You don't want to forget anyone . . . anyone who is important to you."

They had bumped into each other at the school library. Her observation make him think immediately of Cathy. "I've gotten something for my parents, and I'm making individual cards for . . . for friends." He realized he probably would have to include Betty now.

"Oh, can I see? I like to experiment with paint."

"Sure. But they're just pen and ink drawings." He had a folder of sketches and some finished cards. Most were stock images for the season placed in local scenes.

"Oh, they're so nice. If I were a relative, I'd love to get one of these." She held up the First Assembly of God with three wise men before the manger.

"Part of the idea of making gifts is to be economical. College is going to be expensive."

"But college is almost two years away. You have time to save money, and Wesleyan has scholarships. You're sure to be offered one."

Oscar gathered the cards and put them back into the folder. "Well, I have planned a trip to St. Louis while we're visiting my mother's family there next month; and I need money for that.

Besides, I may want to go to college somewhere else. A bigger school, like the university."

Betty frowned. "You're lucky. My parents say I will go to St. Mary's. You don't have to be Catholic, but you do have to attend services. It's very strict."

St. Mary's had recently been accredited and had a strong liberal arts program. But Oscar viewed it as a prison: the girls couldn't leave campus without an escort, always had to be back by nightfall, and received demerits for sloppy dress, unmade beds, failing to observe lights out.

"Professor Lewis thinks there'll be war soon. Maybe none of us will get to go to college. He loaned me a book to read--poems from the First World War. They're so sad." He thought about his uncle back in Jefferson City, whom he'd see in a few weeks.

"Oh, Oscar, if there is a war--and I pray there won't be--don't you go off and volunteer. You have so many talents that . . . that other boys will have to take up the guns and do the fighting."

"I think science is the way to move forward, not conflict." He thought of Thomas Edison, Henry Ford, Madame Curie, recalling encyclopedia stories about their discoveries along with illustrations of the light bulb, the Model T, an X-ray machine. "That's what I'd do, work in weapons research."

"Mr. Hedd says he thinks business is finally picking up, so perhaps other countries won't want

104

to risk losing what they have. And, hey, maybe we'll get a raise!"

"Ha! Not from Mr. Hedd. And it wouldn't help very much anyway. My father and his brothers need a new contract, or he might have to go to work at the sawmill."

"Is there a job? My father never tells me anything about what goes on there."

"They've been asking him to work there since we came to town, but, after he toured the facility, he decided he'd do better on his own--if there's work."

She put her hand on his arm. "I'll pray for him . . . and for you."

While Oscar did worry about the future, his family's financial situation crimped Oscar's expectations primarily in the realm of his romantic life. A teenage boy whose father has always been able to provide for him rarely doubts the future. What Oscar really wondered was how to woo Cathy the horn player without at least some pocket money? Then the perfect idea came to him: a creative representation of music and athleticism.

Oscar tried not to show it, but he was both surprised and thrilled when Cathy accepted his invitation to the movies. All she asked was what time he would pick her up.

"Ah, let's see--the show is at 7:00. I . . . um . . . don't have a car. Is walking okay?"

Ready for cheerleading practice, she was holding a megaphone with the initials SHS embossed in gold. "Yes, just so long as we don't get that storm in Denver. I heard about it on the radio."

Oscar looked at the sky to the west, only some high clouds. Classes were over for the day, and they were standing at the school's back entrance. "I don't think we'll get this one. January's the bad month." It was not always the snow that was difficult to deal with in Salinas, but the wind that whipped across the prairies and cut through even the heaviest coats.

"Okay. I live on West Walnut. Know where that is?"

"You bet. You'll be right on the way . . . from my house." He didn't indicate what street he lived on, worried that she might think his was a poorer neighborhood. She was, after all, the daughter of a doctor. "Let's say, 6:30?" His mind's eye pictured the city map, a route drawn on the straight city streets from home to Walnut to the Orpheum. Where might they go afterwards?

"I'll be ready." Over her shoulder she gave him a big smile as she trotted off to join the other girls on the squad. "And thanks!" As he watched her moving across the grass on those shapely legs, the megaphone firmly gripped in one hand, he felt his Salinas romantic aspirations were at last taking shape--literally and beautifully.

All he had left before pursuing his dream was a lesson with Professor Lewis and his usual work in the shoe store's stock room. After that he'd have time to go home, eat, change clothes, and look sharp . . . as sharp, he believed, as Armand in *Camille*.

He remembered the poster he'd seen downtown featuring two images of Taylor and Garbo. In the larger one, the leading man, his hand gripping the leading lady's bare upper arm, looked deep into her eyes. The heroine's shoulders were exposed, and her head hung back, accenting a bare neck. In the smaller picture, down by a corner, she lay on a bed, and he held her hand.

In part because he was daydreaming of such imagined romantic embraces, his music lesson did not go well. Professor Lewis varied the regular pattern of exercises and asked him to play a series of unusual chords fortissimo. "Let me show you first," he said. As his teacher's hands banged on the keys, the sound grew loud, and the sequence became more and more rapid.

"Ah, I'm not sure I'm ready for this. It's not what I practiced."

Professor Lewis slid his stool to one side to give him room, leaning back with his hands clasped behind his head. "It's just an exercise. Do the best you can."

When Oscar was done, his teacher said, "That's wrist never going to work, is it? At least not to play the piano at the highest level."

"I . . . I had hoped it was just temporary, until it healed. But the doctor says this is the way it's going to be . . . from now on." He raised both hands and inspected them. He had slim, long fingers, though his grip, like his fathers's, was strong.

The doctor had shown him the X-ray and compared it to photographs and diagrams in a medical book. The wrist bone was connected to the arm bone, and the arm bone was connected to the shoulder bone, but the assembly in his case had been damaged.

"Well, there's no reason you can't continue to take lessons. You'll always be . . . competent. Now my newest student, she has genuine promise and is a lot less likely to break bones in fist fights." He pulled his stool back to the piano, juggling the music on the piano. "Anyway, I hear you might be taking up another instrument?"

"Yes, at school, in the band I play the timpani. I like being in the group." What he really liked was the way percussion leads the others.

"Yes, Mrs. Balogh and I talk regularly. No, I meant the saxophone."

"Oh, that. I've just been experimenting. I do like jazz." In his head he heard a riff from Charlie Parker.

When had the image of himself as celebrated musician changed? Back when Professor Lewis, hearing him audition, had agreed to accept him as one of his few town pupils, Oscar imagined himself in the huge concert halls of New York, Paris, Vienna. Now, his fantasy pictured smokey bars and the kind of nightclubs that flourished during Prohibition.

He'd altered his scenario of the future so that, while famous, he was now less conventional. Renowned in smaller, more select circles, his true achievements might only be recognized after he was gone. He would be so far in front of other musicians (or scientists or artists or writers), the world would have to catch up to fully appreciate his genius.

And the women . . . how many of them would regret not admiring his brilliance, failing to seek his affection, missing their one chance to enjoy fulfillment as his lover? Diana, middle-aged and dumpy, wife of a Tank gone to seed, would be the first in a long list to suffer a broken heart.

And now that he thought about Cathy, was she truly close enough to the ideal to enjoy his favor? Could she compare to Greta Garbo, whom he would see that night on the silver screen?

His mother, noticing the way he raced through dinner and dashed up to his room, delayed his chance to find out. "Where will you be this evening?" she asked as he came down from his room. "I had hoped you would stay and listen to *The Scientist's Wife* with us."

She had been become addicted to this soap opera about the home life of a famous research engineer; but she always pretended she was just trying to continue her learning. She might, after all, go back to teaching school one day, she claimed.

"I'm going to the movies, after Bob finishes his milking." This was perhaps true, but he knew from his study of basic logic that the implied causal connection was misleading. "I may have to help, so . . . 'bye."

Oscar was not only eager to be with Catherine in the flesh; but he also had little interest in hearing about the vicarious thrills experienced by a fictional Mary Proud in *The Scientist's Wife*. In a few years, for a college radio skit, he and his best friend Gerry would write a vicious parody about Sissy Tine, *The Proud Wife*. Fortunately, Sallie never heard it.

"You ready?" asked Oscar on Catherine's doorstep.

"Let me just tell my parents I'm on my way." Raising a finger, she left him for a moment and returned almost instantly. Her father was an ophthalmologist, who had developed a successful practice before the Depression began, but he'd had to restrict his operation in the years since then. Still, the family was a clear step up in the social scale from the Lindblooms.

As he walked to the Orpheum with Cathy, he told her the story that inspired the theater's name. He had read about Orpheus, the Greek god of poetry and song, in a book of classical mythology. "The god's lyre," he said, "was more powerful than the Sirens' seductive music, steering a ship's crew away from temptation."

"Oooh! Always beware of sirens," advised Cathy smiling. They were walking briskly as it was cold, though there was no storm on the horizon.

Oscar didn't explain the ultimate fate of Orpheus, who, using his music again, descended into the underworld to rescue his beloved Eurydice. But ignoring a warning not to look back as he fled, Orpheus turned around, and Eurydice disappeared.

"Say, did you buy that saxophone reed?" Cathy asked. "You can be Orpheus and protect other boys from . . . from temptation."

"Hmm. Sometimes it's good to face temptation." He tried to imitate the mature style of the Baron de Varville, who had kept

Camille/Garbo as his mistress. "But I did buy a reed. I just wish I had my own horn, though, because I really love the sound."

"You know so much about music, taking lessons at the college. You'll be better than I am in no time."

"Hmm. If I could rent one, we could practice by playing duets together. What would you think about that?"

"I'd like that, so long as I have the upper part."

"Ah, so you want me to follow you, then. You do know the man's supposed to lead in dancing and . . . in other two-person events."

She turned to look at him, a sly grin on her face. "Sometimes changing things around can be fun. Have you ever played Cat's Cradle?"

"No."

"Well, after the movie, if you want, I'll show you what you can learn with your hands tangled in string!"

If you'd told Oscar that the image of Greta Garbo would fade from his mind almost immediately after the night he saw her as Camille, he would not have believed you. But back in the Rogers' library, all he could see were Catherine's glittering eyes as she worked a long loop of string into different figures. And for days he thought of nothing but how excited he would be to find himself entangled in her charms again.

Oscar was familiar with traditional string figures such as the Cat's Cradle, Jacob's Ladder, and the Osage Two Diamonds; but he was astounded at more complex forms--The Eiffel Tower, the House of the Bos-bird, Two Dolphins.

"There have been string figures at least since Heraklas," explained Cathy, gesturing toward her scrapbook of diagrams and instructions. "He wrote mostly about surgical knots and slings. While his all had medical application, others in Greek society took up the practice of designing and executing complex artistic figures. It was a way to pass the time and to amuse children."

Oscar had his hands extended so she could use some of his fingers as additional anchor points for the construction of what she called her most ambitious conception. "I figured they only started when we had kite string lying around the house after a windy day."

His father had made many kites for Oscar over the years, most in the traditional diamond shape but others more sophisticated and complex. Carl explained how he and his brothers had made them out of sticks and discarded newspaper. They would wait for strong but cold sea breezes and compete with their box kites, delta kits, and roller kites. The sport inspired innovative design and hands-on execution.

"Flying kites is an old custom, too," Cathy explained. "String for making figures came from fishermen, who had lots for the making of nets. Women, of course, have been sewing for as far back in time as anyone can imagine, so they've always had thread on hand. Making designs out of string is really universal: Eskimos do it, pygmies in Africa do it, South Sea islanders, Indians, Europeans."

"I'm surprised it's not mentioned in the Bible."

"I don't know about that, but my minister says when he was a missionary in China, he used string figures to teach concepts of the Church."

"Well, there is a cross . . . " He was suddenly worried that Cathy would turn out to be as religious as Betty, less interested in his body than his soul. He was pleased that she shifted the subject back to the secular realm.

"Making string figures can be therapeutic, too. It's calming and gives you a sense of satisfaction. Farmers can use cord to bind a hoe

114

blade to a staff or hogtie sheep for sheering, knowing what they've done will help provide for their families in the future."

"If I were preaching to natives in Africa, though, I'd worry about them taking my string and tying me up in a pot to boil for stew!"

She laughed. "Oh, that's the way with you boys, always making weapons out of toys. If I let you have this, you want to make a bow and start shooting arrows at tiny birds."

Oscar was feeling more like a bound sheep than the predator wolf, as she slipped another loop around the thumb on his left hand. "Be a little more charitable," he urged. "Not everything men make has to be utilitarian. Maybe some of my male ancestors were thinking of stringed instruments--Orpheus' lyre, for instance--to calm the savage beast and lure children to sleep at night." He wondered if his Swedish ancestor had made his own clarinet.

"Perhaps, but they would have been the rare members of the species. Men like to build things with sticks and stones or pound things into oblivion with stones and sticks. It's the girls who add beauty to the world."

Oscar had to admit to feeling satisfaction at his perfectly executed downing of Tank at the county fair, but he also hoped he would build aesthetically pleasing constructions in words and musical notes. "You ought to hear Jackson--he works at Wesleyan--plays the saxophone. You'd feel differently then about men."

"He's a professor?" She lisped the word "professor" because she had a length of string held between her teeth. It would be a part of her grand conception, but Oscar had no clue what part or what construction.

"No, . . . uh, he tunes the pianos and keeps all the instruments in working order. But he has his own jazz combo that plays at . . . plays downtown." He was aware that the Hi-Hat didn't have the best reputation. It had been a speakeasy during Prohibition, and it was not uncommon now for brawls to break out on weekend nights or holidays.

"Hmm. Is he that Negro I heard about? Mother thinks he shouldn't be allowed in the Sunflower." The Hi-Hat was, ironically, in a basement room of what was once Salinas' premier hotel, strategically located by Union Station. The bar's entrance was by an outside stairway in the alley, just off the main street.

"I don't know anything about that. I just overheard him in the music building one day after my piano lesson. He sounded as good as the best horn players you hear on the radio, and I'd love to hear him perform." Minors were not allowed in the Hi-Hat.

There were few African-Americans in Salinas in those years, and Oscar didn't recognize the rigid, unofficial lines of separation that existed

116

within his own community. Those growing up in other parts of the country saw signs for "White" and "Colored," but he would have understood such designations as referring to shades of red, green, yellow, blue, and all of them together.

"Well, Negroes don't build anything, so he's not anyone you could point to using string for positive purposes."

Oscar thought about how quickly Jackson had identified and remedied the problem with Professor Lewis' piano, which, after all, had quite a few strings to it--not just the ones struck by hammers to make sound, but others that stitched together little components to connect the movement of fingers to the production of sound.

"So, tell me again what we're making here?" He nodded, as there were no fingers remaining on either of his hands to point to the matrix of crossing and crisscrossing string linking the two of them together.

"This, dear boy, is a model of the human eye--retina, pupil, iris, optical nerve, lens, ciliar muscle--every part of the intricate, complex organism."

"I . . . I didn't see it." He hoped she would take this as a joke.

"You're not the daughter of an ophthalmologist. But I am, and this is what I'm going to show him for Christmas."

"Right." Oscar hiked his upper lip to raise the glasses on his nose, indicating that her father was correcting his vision with them. "I'm just one of his patients."

Cathy pulled his hands closer to the string eyeball and moved her head beside it. "You could, though, be my patient one day."

"I could?"

She nodded. "Sure, in a kind of game, I mean. I bet you've played doctor with the girls before. This time I would be the nurse, and you would have . . . um . . . a sore leg, an injury, maybe from fighting another boy. I would have to, you know, examine you."

"Well . . . "

"Because you would be kind of in shock, even though you won the fight. You always win your fights, don't you? But I would tell you to lie down with your feet elevated, just in case. I'd put a wet cloth over your forehead and eyes to calm you."

"Well . . . "

"Then, I'd begin my examination. You wouldn't be nervous, would you?"

A health class diagram of the human muscular, vascular, and nervous systems flashed into his mind. Nerves animating limbs; blood feeding tissue; muscles lifting bones. What, exactly, would she been examining?

"Well . . . "

118

"After all," she went on, "we've already been out on a date. And we've been sharing a musical instrument. You have your reed, and I have mine; but there's only one mouthpiece. And we've . . . put our lips and tongues on it. So, it would be okay if I touched you . . . as a nurse."

Oscar was afraid he was already going into shock.

So, this was it: the conquest he'd dreamed of ever since he'd learned about the nature of adult love. And he wouldn't even have to be the aggressor. She was coming to him!

Of course, he, the powerful man, would take over from her, the weaker female, at some point. He would pull up from his prone position, take her by her shoulders, roll her onto her back as Tarzan crushed Jane in his arms, as Count Vronsky overwhelmed Anna Karinina, as Robert Taylor swept Greta Garbo up in his embrace.

It might happen as early as the following weekend. There was going to be a Saturday practice for the winter band concert, a fundraiser for the spring band trip to Lawrence. Cathy asked him to walk her home afterwards.

"Sometimes I don't take the straightest route, you know," she had said with a wink. He looked at her and raised one eyebrow. In his head he began to chart paths on a map of the city that went by vacant lots, quiet parks, the back corners of the college campus. He also envisioned ways in which he might find himself in need of fictional medical attention.

Oscar tried to sound sensible even as he gave her the opportunity to back away. "It might be dark by that time, and that snow you were worried about is forecast for the weekend."

"Let's take our chances. I know a few places where we can slip out of the wind, if we need to."

"Out of the wind and into something more comfortable?" thought Oscar, recalling many a risqué story he'd heard but not daring to speak the words out loud. His response, though, left room for the same suggestion. "I'll plan for a possible detour." This time he added a wink of his own.

The rendezvous would be even more convenient for him than taking Catherine to see *Camille* had been. For that date, he'd disguised his exact plans from his mother, letting her incorrectly extend his statement that he might help Bob milk his goats to an assertion that they would be going to the movies together. Now he would simply be attending band practice, which might last . . . oh, you never know with Mrs. Balogh.

The new director had been even more intense than usual in the last few weeks, keeping the students past the official end of class time. Bob told Oscar on their morning walk to school that he was worried about her. "She seems unfocused, or maybe distracted, when she talks about the music, composers, history. But then when she conducts . . . it's like another person."

Oscar, feeling he knew something about the artistic temperament, explained: "Musicians are that way. They come alive with the music. It takes them away from gritty reality to a better world."

He thought of himself wailing away on a tenor sax, lost in an improvisation of "Caravan," translated into a clean desert landscape with an angelic female companion.

"I think it has something to do with her family back in Europe," Bob insisted. "I . . . um, overheard her talking to Mrs. Bass about the 'Rome-Berlin Axis,' whatever that is."

Mrs. Bass was the school's history teacher. Like Professor Lewis, she was worried about the rise of Fascism in Germany and Italy. She had a son in the Army; and, with her knowledge of what had happened in the First World War, she feared another global conflict that would eventually draw America out of its isolation.

"Professor Lewis told me about it. He said it was all the alliances knitting countries together that made war unavoidable the last time. If one was attacked, the rest had already committed to come to their defense. It's happening again, and Germany is strengthening its military at the same time."

"Well, I think Mr. Balogh is in Poland or somewhere like that, trying to join his wife in this country. For some reason, he isn't being allowed to leave."

Oscar snorted. "Well, that's far away from here and not something we can do anything about. I'm more interested in girls located in Salinas, Kansas, who might want to make alliances with local boys."

122

"Oh, going after Diana again?"

"No, she belongs to Tank. But Cathy Rogers is teaching me to play the saxophone, and I don't object to being in her company."

`"You lucky dog! She's got a mighty nice build, and I hear she let Martin go pretty far before they split up." He put his palms together in an attitude of prayer. "You know those Catholics can always get forgiveness for . . . for letting an ally get pretty close."

Oscar was ready to believe his friend about Catherine's past and to conclude that this boded well for his future. But his confidence in himself and his prospects were shaken the day before his second date with the attractive cheerleader.

Waiting for his music lesson outside Professor Lewis' office, he heard a remarkably skilled performance. "That must be his new star student," Oscar thought. "Good, but not a true virtuoso." He admired technical brilliance, perhaps more than musical beauty.

Sitting on a bench, he looked--as he always did--up and down the hall. Carol, the attractive student who'd told him about *Lady Chatterley's Lover*, might show up again. He remembered how she'd slid along the bench closer and closer to him. Finally, it seemed her tongue had touched his ear as she whispered that she did ". . . a lot . . . of . . . reading."

He turned back to the office door, cracked open a few inches. The Chopin (etude no.5 op.10) was not that challenging technically, but he had to admit it was being performed with an unusually gifted touch.

When it was over, he could hear Professor Lewis praising the student, making only a few critical comments. The door opened halfway, and Oscar saw a slender young woman with a heavy winter coat backing out. She paused with one hand on the doorknob, listening to her teacher's final comments. He was no longer talking about music.

"I'm sorry to learn what your cousin has written, but it confirms some of my own fears. If countries choose to close their eyes, the rest of us are going to have a hard time of it."

The slender blonde student responded, "She writes that at least more Jews are being allowed to come into the country, but they do tell terrible stories of what they experienced in their homelands. My father says those things aren't happening, and I want to believe him."

"People around here either think nothing is happening or, if it is, it has little to do with them-- it's all Old World troubles. But I read that Lindbergh is visiting Germany again to learn about their airplane and rocket technology. These things--and any weapons they might carry--can end the separation of the United States from the rest of the world in a matter of hours."

She shook her head. "My uncle, who was in the Swedish army, says we have to stay out of wars."

"Well, let's not spoil your excellent lesson with dark thoughts right now about what's going on elsewhere. Keep practicing, but no more than the amount I've set. You can cause damage by overdoing the exercises at this point. And you have a bright future."

"Thank you, Professor. Thank you ever so much." Ducking her head shyly, she backed the rest of way out of the office and pulled the door shut behind her. When she turned and saw Oscar, she smiled and blushed. "Oh, Oscar. Hello. I didn't think I'd see you here."

"Hi . . . Elsa. Ah, yes, I . . . I take lessons from Professor Lewis, too. But I didn't know you did."

"Oh, I just started. I learned from Mrs. Olson, our church organist. But she recommended I find a more experienced teacher. And he . . . " she gestured to the door, "oh, he's marvelous!"

"I'm a new student, too--at least here. And, as you know, I broke my wrist at the fair. That's slowed me a bit." He paused. "Well, nice to see you. I'd better go in. It's my time." He gestured toward the office.

"Of course. Well, I'll probably see you here again--maybe next week. Or in Assyria . . . ?"

"Perhaps." He almost went on to say he thought another consultation among the brothers

125

had been planned and that he'd be coming with his father. But her obvious eagerness to see him was making him uncomfortable. Next to Catherine, she seemed so young and innocent.

He didn't see his cousin that weekend, though, because of what he learned when he arrived at Hedd's after this lesson. Betty came out of the stock room to tell him she was taking his place that afternoon.

"Go to the hospital right now," she said with a look of alarm. "It's your mother."

Chapter Eighteen: Draw

If it were true that bad things come in threes, Oscar feared what might be around the corner that winter. It looked as if his father was going to have to go to work for the sawmill in a role which compromised his high standards as a craftsman. And Dr. Johnson couldn't say what his mother's problem was, only that she had suffered some kind of "collapse" while hanging clothes out in the cold December wind. What else threatened Oscar's future?

When he found his father at the hospital, he learned that, while his mother was "resting comfortably" now, she would have to stay for several days of tests and to recover her strength. "She has been working too hard," Carl explained.

"It's because . . . jobs are so tight, isn't it?" Oscar asked. "And she's taking on extra customers." He didn't want to say that his father might actually be out of work. And he didn't want to acknowledge that, even though she never asked him, he could have been helping his mother more with her laundry. "I know she's been worried that we might not make the trip back to Jefferson City." Oscar also worried that his own excursion to St. Louis might be canceled.

"Ja, it's those things for sure. I told her I would take the job at Bensons' and that made her relax some. We will have steady money."

"But you don't want to work for them, do you?" Carl had told him the paychecks would come regularly--so long as the mill itself continued to operate--but that his tasks would be dull and repetitive. He did not like it that he would not have control of the final product.

"Sometimes, son, you have take on some things you don't like. The banks are not loaning money, and your uncles and I haven't been able to find a new project." They had been building small barns for farmers who had enjoyed good wheat crops the last few years.

Oscar's understanding of business was remarkably innocent, especially for one so perceptive in other areas. With an unchallenged belief in his father's abilities, he saw their future within a distorted frame of a Monopoly game: you started with a sum of money, came upon prospects, and went from poverty to spectacular wealth in very little time. Loans to finance projects, land to put structures on, lumber to build with were positioned inside a neat rectangular grid of Salinas streets and sectioned Kansas farms. Chance moved you from opportunity to opportunity along a path to success.

He didn't see the omissions such a pattern obscured nor the forces outside that frame that might transform the entire system. While he acknowledged setbacks from time to time for individual players, Oscar's confidence in his quiet, steady father had led him to assume a regular accumulation of property and the growth of capital as other, less able competitors faced bankruptcy, sickness, failure.

So, when Betty told him later that she was praying for his family, he wondered why she thought it was necessary. Even his father's admission that there could be more to his mother's sickness "this time" hadn't registered at first with Oscar as completely as it should have.

He did ask his father, "This time? She's been sick like this before?"

Carl rubbed his forehead and brought his fingers down across his eyes. "Long ago, before you came to us, she . . . would be unwell from time to time. We never knew exactly what the cause was, and since she's had you to take care of, she has felt well."

Oscar thought of Camille, slowing dying of a terrible disease. He tried to recall his mother showing symptoms--tiredness, coughing, going pale. There had been none of that.

His father was reassuring. "She will recover. Go in and speak to her for just a moment. She will want to know you are here. Tomorrow we will find her much better."

Oscar was comforted by his mother's smile, though he could see how tired she was in the lines of her face and by the way she closed her eyes while he spoke. But her assurance that she "had just gotten over tired" allowed him to leave her sleeping an hour later.

And when he went in to work Saturday morning before band practice, he brushed aside Betty's worry. "She's been getting better every day. She just pushed herself, that's all."

"You need to be careful yourself. Don't take on too much . . . or too many . . . activities. You'll need to help both your parents."

He put on his work gloves to start sweeping and mopping the stockroom floor. "She's improving. Today she was reading in bed and planning how to recover our sofa. Like everyone else these days, she just works hard to help provide for the family."

Betty moved some empty boxes out of his way. "I guess I'm lucky. Benson's seems to continue its operation. Daddy says they have been finding new customers overseas."

"He should know; he's the bookkeeper." Oscar realized that soon he and Betty would have more in common, their fathers working at the same place. "But you're helping out, too. I think more and more girls are getting part time jobs instead of . . . of volunteering." He almost said, " . . . instead of taking part in church activities." He didn't want to bring up the subject of religion, as he knew it would turn to the question of his own salvation.

She shrugged. "I like to work here so I can be away from home now and then. My parents are

130

pretty strict. Anyway, I'm glad I could substitute for you this week."

"I'll return the favor. Just let me know when you want to skip a Saturday."

"You can do me a favor right now. Will you look at the painting I did for my parents' Christmas?"

"Sure. I didn't know you painted." He recalled showing her the pen and ink drawings he was using as gifts this year. Her painting might be a kind of response.

Betty went to the little closet where they hung up their coats for work. She pulled a sheet of heavy watercolor paper out of a large brown envelope. He was struck immediately by the color--bright oranges, yellows, and reds--and by the central figure.

"That's beautiful!" he said, though there was more than skill revealed in what he saw. The painting was realistic, not what he expected from a girl whose focus was often on the hereafter. Animals and people had genuine physical presence in a holy scene.

"Thank you. I liked the subject. Can you guess what inspired it?"

Oscar shook his head as he continued to examine it. The images were traditional: the angel before the shepherds with a star high above the scene. But two things fascinated him: the transcendent light around the angel's face and the very earthly beauty of her womanly form.

"I thought the angel was a man."

"Well, usually he is. But I had a reason to do something different."

"Hmm. Was it a photograph you worked from? Or a magazine picture?"

"No. Nothing like that. The idea came from a story I heard, a story your mother told me a few weeks ago."

He studied the scene once more. While there were the usual sheep and fields, a night sky with one prominent star, shepherds gazing in wonder, they all faded before the striking figure of the angel, whose robes clung to her body in a very un-angelic way. (Bob would have said she had "a mighty nice figure." A church commentator might have been struck by her "ample bosom.")

"My mother? Isn't that curious. What did she say?"

"She told me about one Christmas on the farm when she was growing up. She woke very early and, rather than go downstairs to the see the tree with presents arranged around it, she looked out her window across the pasture to the east. The sun was breaking through some low clouds, and she said she could almost see individual beams shining toward her."

"There's a good, long view from the house's second story after the leaves have fallen."

Betty held the painting up and studied it. "Mrs. Lindbloom told me she saw a figure in the light, an angel, she believed. And the angel spoke to her. She told her one day she would have a son, a son who would . . . " She looked away from Oscar, but he could see Betty was blushing. " . . . who would be very beautiful and do wonderful things."

Oscar tried to make light of his mother's feelings . . . and Betty's. "Ha! She would be disappointed in that!"

She slid the picture back into the envelope. "I . . . I don't think so." He wondered if she understood the angel she had painted was a profound representation of beauty. "Anyway. I do hope my parents like it."

Oscar assured her they would like because it was indeed well done, and it embodied their beliefs. What the picture embodied for him, however, was a strikingly real female, a vibrant, sensual being whose high breasts, rich auburn hair, and parted lips did not appear in the usual representation of a heavenly visitor. They belonged, he realized with new appreciation, to Betty herself.

When he arrived at the Saturday band practice a few hours later, still bemused by Betty's unexpected attractiveness, Oscar found the auditorium unusually quiet. Most of the students were seated with their instruments and talking softly, though the session wasn't scheduled to begin for another ten minutes. Then he saw the reason for the uncharacteristically subdued crowd: Wesleyan College's Jackson was in the percussion section.

The races were generally separated into groups at school functions, so it was unusual for Jackson, though an adult, to be in the auditorium with the band, which had no black members. Oscar assumed he had been called in to tune or adjust some of the instruments. And, having seen him often at the college, he didn't register the event as particularly significant.

Listening to big bands on the radio, he had learned that Benny Goodman caused a bit of a stir by integrating his orchestra. But such events, transmitted over the airwaves, happened in a distant world with its separate reality, and Oscar didn't connect them to his school or his town.

He also noticed Professor Lewis off in one corner, listening intently to Mrs. Balogh, who was showing him what looked to be a letter. Talking energetically, she held it open with one hand and after a minute slapped it flatly with the back of her other hand, as if to say maybe that this was an affront of some sort or perhaps that this was a senseless piece of writing.

Oscar was primarily interested, of course, in locating the pretty girl with the saxophone. As he mounted the steps to the back platform where the timpani were set up, he smiled at her. Catherine was sitting in the middle of the horn section. And she smiled in return.

Finding Jackson kneeling at his drums, he asked, "Is there a problem?"

"Rods need adjusting."

Oscar was adept at setting the gauges, which must be done before any performance to compensate for humidity, temperature, changing weather conditions. But adjusting the tuning rods around the edge of the drum was beyond his expertise. Mrs. Balogh must have heard something odd and called in Jackson. The band was to be working on the new piece by Mrs. Balogh's countryman, and Oscar knew she wanted the premier performance to be perfect.

Watching Jackson refine the instruments, he thought of how he might fine tune his patter for Cathy on the walk home, especially if they did play patient and nurse as she had hinted. He admired the clever dialogue of Clark Gable in *Love on the Run*. In one sequence the star and Joan Crawford attempt to determine where they are by comparing the colors on a map with the

135

geography they see from the air: a pinkish brown means one country and a shade of green is another.

Again, Oscar recalled a health class, pull-down chart of the human body's circulatory, muscular, skeletal, and nervous systems. "Where does it hurt, darling?" Joan Crawford asks in his imagination.

"It was hurting there, but once you touched it, it got better," replies Clark.

"How about here?"

"Umm. That's improving remarkably. Perhaps you should continue the treatment."

Moving closer, she suggests, "Perhaps I need a more direct view of . . . of . . . the area."

"The cause of medical science should not be impeded by . . . by . . . something so insubstantial as . . . trousers," he whispers.

Ending up where smooth talk was called for, it turned out, was as easy as Oscar had hoped. After the intense practice session, his fellow band members were eager to get on with their usual weekend activities; and Oscar and Cathy ended up being nearly the last to leave. Bundled up against the cold, they walked away from school more as if they were simply headed the same way rather than that they were bent on heady experimentation.

"You know," she told him, "we'll pass my father's office going this way."

"Oh? I don't see . . . "

"Sure, you turn here, go three blocks, turn back west." She winked. "And I am feeling a bit chilly, so perhaps we could duck in there for a few minutes to warm ourselves up."

"Now I see! You have a key?"

"Yes, I work there from time to time. But no one will be in today. Father and Mother were driving over to Manhattan. She wanted to do some shopping, and he was going to the university library. I saw to it that the heat would be on."

"Well, a few minutes out of . . . out of the wind makes sense to me."

"As we warm up, we can do that nursing exam I told you about." She raised an eyebrow, "It will raise the temperature, too, you know."

He did. Or he thought he did. But it did other things he didn't anticipate.

The ophthalmologist's daughter had him sit in one of the customary examining chairs facing an eye chart across the room. She pulled a stool on wheels over to arrange him and the equipment: his feet on a rest extended from the base of the chair, his forehead pressed into something like binoculars at the end of a metal arm, his hands on two armrests.

Slipping off the stool, she dimmed all the lights except one that focused on the chart, almost a spotlight. Over the next few minutes, she then asked, "Which is clearer, this? Or this?" Again, "Which is clearer, this? Or this?" And again, "Which is clearer, this? Or this?"

What he saw was Cathy in her coat, Cathy out of her coat; Cathy in her sweater; Cathy out of her sweater; Cathy in her blouse; Cathy out of her blouse. The fewer the clothes, the clearer he declared his vision to be.

"Now," she said, smiling, "now, we need to do another test."

His voice was husky. "I'm . . . ready. What do I do?" He didn't sound as sophisticated as Clark Cable. Actually, he just hoped he wasn't drooling on the chin rest of the goggle apparatus!

"Well, your vision is fine, but I need to check the other senses. Touch, for instance." She came up beside him. "The senses are all interconnected, you know. Each system contributes to the others, creating the complete entity. Can you read the third line of letters?"

He stared ahead at the chart across the room: "E D F C Z P." He named each one from left to right but read the line to himself as "Ed fools zee police."

"Very good. Keep looking, but tell me if you feel this."

He felt her hand on his knee and said, "Yes. Yes, I do."

"Read the next line, please."

"F E L O P Z D." In his mind, he read the letters as "feel oh please!"

The hand slid half way up his thigh. "This?"

Again he said, "Yes."

"The next line?"

"Ah, it's a bit hard . . . but I think, 'D E F P O T E C'" This time his voice was a whisper, and the letters spelled no message.

Cathy leaned closer and spoke more softly, her mouth close to his ear. "How about this?"

His "Yes" was barely audible, and he didn't try to read the next row, though he couldn't have anyway. It was one of the few moments in his life where his nearsightedness didn't matter.

Somewhere in the back of his mind, Oscar realized it was time for him to reverse roles, to become the leader, the man who takes charge. She, Deja Thoris, shouldn't be the one making advances on him, John Carter of Mars. But he was caught in the examining chair with a lens device pressed against his forehead, the back of his head blocked by a head rest. Too, her hand was keeping his pelvis in the chair.

He tried to think if, with a single sweep of his own hand--not unlike the right cross he had delivered to Tank--he might brush aside the goggle device, then swing his legs from the footrest and rise up over a suddenly meeker Catherine. Taking her in an embrace, his hand would go to the analogous place on her that hers had been on him. She would go weak in his arms, and he would take things from there to their logical conclusion. It needed but the decision to act.

That decision came in the next instant, as he realized what she was doing was dangerously close to arriving at an outcome he would find embarrassing, sloppy, unromantic indeed. Panicking, he did what he'd imagined: sweep, rise, embrace, grab. He was relieved immediately that he had been able to act but just as quickly shocked at the result.

His hand had reached its target with unerring accuracy, as if he had done this many times, though it was the first. The satisfaction of power and control he had anticipated, however, exploded as he came in contact with the unexpected reality of a girl who had become excited--very excited.

"It's wet!" he cried, almost with horror. It didn't help a bit to recall her earlier assertion that the human body is 99% water.

That night Oscar went back to the books. After all he'd read, how was it possible he knew so little about a girl's physical response to . . . to . . . to a boy's touch? He'd studied medical books, books on "feminine hygiene," even books about the reactions of female athletes to stress, exertion, sustained, intense activity. Surely, some of them could have included references to the physiological reality he experienced with Cathy. Something must have been left out.

He thought about his friend's goats and the male animal's enormous appetite in mounting. "The buck in rut is a machine," Bob had told him. They were standing outside the pen, watching the buck brought in as stud spread his urine on his legs and face.

"Well, Billy has a whole herd to satisfy, so I guess he'd better have energy. But why he wants to stink himself up is beyond me."

"The does won't have anything to do with him unless he does," explained Bob. Oscar had only been thinking of Billy's actions and feelings. What Sleepy and Bashful wanted from Billy, and what they did to receive him, had never occurred to him.

At home that night, he recalled Carol, the Wesleyan coed who'd told him about *Lady Chatterley's Lover*, almost, he felt, putting her

141

tongue in his ear. He pulled his copy of the novel from its hiding place under the attic bedroom floor. (He'd lifted out a short board in one corner of the room and used a bent nail both to hold it loosely in place and to serve as a handle.) Perhaps there was an answer here.

He read again the account of Michael's first time with Connie. One look from him, Lawrence wrote, had struck her so strongly that it "affected her direct in the womb." He had wondered exactly what that meant when he first read it, but satisfied his curiosity then by concluding she'd felt some sort of contraction or spasm.

He turned to the worn pages of Chapter 10, where the keeper finds Lady Chatterley moved by the power of animal instinct. When he touches her, first in a kind of compassion, she responds with confusion. Then, as his hand travels to "the curve of her crouching loins," she is soon "blindly trying to dry her face." Later, Oscar read, after they lay together, that she is aware of his "wet body" touching hers.

Well, he decided, it might have been there all along; he just hadn't read between the lines. It was too late now, of course, to change his reaction to Cathy in her father's office. Miraculously, she had not seemed offended, though the spell of the pretend examination was certainly broken.

"Hah," she had gasped, freeing himself from his embrace. "I guess we've warmed up enough!" She put her fingers in her hair and flipped it away

142

from her face. "And, I'm happy to report that all your senses are normal."

Oscar was straightening his trousers, which had been bunched up during the examination. "Yes, and I must say you conducted the tests rather well." He gestured toward the wall. "The charts . . . the lens . . . . the, um, instructions. So, maybe we should both get home before it's too late in the day."

"Yes, home now. My parents will be back soon. But Oscar . . . ?"

"Yes?"

"I hope you'll keep coming around . . . to borrow my horn and . . . maybe learn some new string figures with me."

"Sure, sure! In fact, I've found out about an especially challenging design an aunt of my mine wrote me about. And I'm going to see if I can find an old saxophone for myself. I might like the alto sax more, now that I think about it. We could play some interesting duets."

They would not play many duets, it turned out, though they were entangled in one more intricate string fantasy. Cathy's family moved to Manhattan before winter was over, apparently for business reasons. By then, Oscar had been to Missouri and encountered another beautiful woman who would represent the ideal for him throughout his college years and beyond. The eye examination marked a threshold in his sexual awakening, but one he would not cross completely for several more years.

After a few days Cathy reminded him that the human body contains a lot of water, his father gave him more information about a woman's make-up, this time about the emotional and psychological nature of the sex.

Oscar was in the garage experimenting with the alto saxophone Bob had found in an uncle's attic. Carl had come in by the side door and was leaning up against his workbench. Oscar could tell he was exhausted, not necessarily from overwork but from a combination of physical effort and mental strain.

"That bad at Bensons'?"

"Bad? Ja, the day does not make me feel proud. I cut with this bandsaw from early until late, logs turning into lumber. But what comes from the lumber I never see. It is graded, packaged, and shipped to somewhere else, perhaps overseas."

"I read they are using less wood in manufacturing--it's all steel, now."

"Yes, but that is not all that causes me sadness, Oscar. I must tell you something else."

"Mother's not still sick, is she?"

"No, it's not that. Her strength is fine. She is eating well and will soon be completely back in her routine, so long as . . . " Carl paused, rubbed his forehead, bringing his fingers down across his eyes. To Oscar it looked as if he were embarrassed, but his father never did anything that would need apology or explanation.

"So long as ... ?"

"We must not have her get excited, Oscar. That is what caused this sickness. It was what your friend Betty did."

"Betty? She and Mother get along so well. And Mother and Mrs. Devine share ... a number of interests." He didn't want to say the interest of religion, though he knew all three of these women were concerned about the state of their souls--and his.

"That is true. And Betty did not mean to make her upset. But she told her you were thinking about going early away to college, maybe even out of the state."

Oscar thought back to the conversation he'd had with her when he had showed her his handmade Christmas cards. "Ah. I guess we did talk about that."

"Ja, well, that is what made your mother to worry." He paused. "You know that she had you moved ahead in school, skipping the second grade because you were far ahead of your classmates. So, you are already a year younger than others in your class. If you jump ahead ... "

"But I've always been the best in my class, even if I'm a year younger."

"That I know. But it doesn't make your mother easy. She is an intense person. You know that. And this idea that you would be away from home, with older people who might take advantage, it grew with her. It got to be such a concern that she . . . she became . . . nervous."

Oscar realized he was not using the term, "a nervous breakdown," but that must be what his mother suffered from. "And this had happened before . . . ?"

"Yes, we were married, you know, for some years before you came to us. We did not know why . . . a child did not come before. Her brother Sam, now, he has his three. And my brothers and sisters--you have many cousins. After some years went by, it worried her."

"But I'm here now. I'll always be her son. If I was away at school, I would write. I would visit. Would she really want me to spend my whole life in Salinas?"

Carl shook his head. "Oscar, it is not she who asks you remain here. It is I who make this request. You can start at the college next fall, if they will admit you. And after college we will see. But, if you were to go away now, I would be too afraid for your mother's health."

Oscar looked again at his father's stoic face. The lines around his eyes told how he had faced hardships: the loss of his parents at an early age, the struggle to get what schooling he could in his

146

native country, emigration to America to start with nothing.

"I understand, Father. I won't speak of going away again." He adjusted the music before him and tried to look cheerful. "It's exciting enough to think I'll start college in the fall!"

In his heart, though, he felt a strong contraction. The worlds of concert performance, movie stardom, a scientist's university laboratory were suddenly less within reach. The chance to win a beautiful woman sought by many men had shrunk. And, ironically, these were the goals his mother had instilled in him from an early age. Now she was making them impossible.

But Oscar would learn that he was discounting changes outside his immediate experience that would determine the course of his future. History was generating a global conflict into which he and many he held dear would be drawn. It would also bring him his bride.

Interlude: Building

When two of Oscar's children visited the Show Me state a few years after his death, they searched for buildings important to family history. It had been decades since they'd been in the state capitol, where their grandparents had lived, or in St. Louis, where their father once spent a memorable two days in the winter of his last year in high school. The trip filled in an important chapter in their parents' story--or almost did.

While their mother would live another ten years, she seemed to know surprisingly little of Oscar's young adulthood, that time before he, as a recent college graduate, boldly introduced himself to her. Within a week he had declared that he was the man of her dreams.

Marian did think, though, that Oscar's earlier excursion to St. Louis had been important. For one thing he found himself on Route 66, road of opportunity. And once he had accepted the fact that he wouldn't be going away to school, he took this two-day visit as a foretaste of adventure to follow. He relished the city streets, tall buildings, busy crowds of aspiring workers.

Nana also had a vague recollection that Oscar was settled in unexpected ways by what happened there, preparing him for his successful transition to college the next fall. His mother's recovery improved after she got to see her parents and other relatives. That, in turn, helped Carl, her husband; and the household was more peaceful that year and the next.

Curtis and Carol's guide for their two-city trip was an annotated sketch book they had found among Oscar's office papers from South Central Missouri State University. But the children knew their father was a storyteller who liked to disguise his opinion. The truth would be in his anecdote or reminiscence, but elusive, shifting, open to interpretation. It was one of the contradictions in his character: a scientist committed to empirical knowledge, he also was drawn to the possibilities of such things as palm reading, gypsy fortune-telling, ghostly visitation.

First among their stops were the two houses build by their grandfather, Carl Lindbloom, for his young family and his wife's parents. Side-by-side modest structures, their style revealed their age (nearly 100 years) but their appearance showed lasting craftsmanship.

"Why do you suppose he never pointed them out to us?" Curt, the middle sibling of the family, asked. "We probably came here to see Grandma and Grandpa fifty times growing up, but I don't recall his ever mentioning them. He lived here for his first nine years."

Carol, a scientist like her father, had never been particularly interested in such matters. "It's interesting to see that it's still standing, but we all grow up somewhere."

149

"Yes, but don't you think the structures around you shape you in some ways?"

"No."

Wider than the traditional shotgun house, these two were positioned perpendicularly to the street with living room in front, bedrooms behind them, and kitchens in the rear. The ground sloped away from the street, so the back of the house was one story up from ground level. There was a view all the way to high bluffs above the Missouri River at the center of town.

Curtis said, "I can see how such simple design and functionality could have inspired Dad's interest with architecture. He might well have continued in Grandpa's profession, though at a level removed from actual building, if the war hadn't intervened."

"He could have come back to it, if he'd wanted to. Let's see this other house." She was holding the sketch book. "Who did you say lived there?"

"His Aunt Agnes. Don't you remember anything?"

Carol shrugged. "Only if it's nontrivial. Was she the one who ran the restaurant?"

"Right. On McCartney Street, off Broadway, I think. Look," Curtis gestured. "You can see down this hill and up the other hill--that's High Street up there."

"I thought the important thing was that he stayed with her after he graduated from college--looking for work in--when was it?--'41?"

Aunt Agnes had run a breakfast/lunch diner catering to downtown workers and government employees. In a house next door to the restaurant she also cared for her husband John, invalided in World War I. Even Carol acknowledged that she was a strong woman, ahead of her time.

Curt did not tell her about the odd drawing he'd found tucked in the sketchbook with a note, "Aunt Agnes." It was a string figure design that, viewed one way, represented a saxophone; but, turned upside down and around, it resembled a woman bending over in a provocative pose.

"Must have been '42. He met Mom the next year, and they were married by summer."

The diner and neighboring house, it turned out, were gone, replaced by parking lots as downtown fought the growth of shopping centers on the edges of the city. So, they made a quick run by the house they had visited as children, a simple two-room building with a cabinet shop attached on one side. It had been remodeled, the shop converted into part of the living area.

They also understood, though, that in St. Louis were other models for their father's architectural ambitions. His two days there in the winter, before he enrolled at Salinas Wesleyan, gave him reasons to dream on a grander scale. And Carol and Curtis would tour them in a few days, before one flew east and the other west to their respective homes.

Throughout their stay in Missouri, though, they were haunted by the sense that there was more to this story than they were finding, just as there had always seemed to be a missing element in their understanding of their parents' courtship. Oscar and Marian had explained how they met at the Board of Health sixty years earlier, but the children had sometimes caught them giving each other knowing winks whenever they recounted that event.

When Curtis reported on this trip, his mother seemed less interested in what they saw in Jefferson City, where she had met Oscar, than their experiences in St. Louis. "What did you find around Memorial Plaza area?" she asked, as if there were something special to be seen there. "Perhaps some novel shops?"

"To be honest," Curtis admitted, "we didn't spend much time in that area. We saw the Soldiers' Memorial, but I doubt if Dad would have taken much interest in that." It commemorated World War I veterans. "We went to the buildings in his sketchbook."

She shrugged, as if they should understand. Later Curt went back to the sketch book to see if he'd overlooked any little shops but found only references to large, historical structures.

Oscar had been impressed by The Arena, a new entertainment center at the time, second in size only to Madison Square Garden. Its cantilever steel trusses supporting a lamella roof made interior columns unnecessary, generating uninterrupted views from all angles. It was the kind of stage on which Oscar felt he belonged. Circumnavigating it by foot that January day, he thought about how narrow the field of his endeavors had been and how great was his ambition.

He also wrote about The Jewel Box, an Art-Deco floral conservatory that had only been open a few weeks when Oscar toured the city. Its roof of wood planking, horizontal metal surfaces, and vertical walls that include 4000 panes of glass framed by copper with a verdigris patina were full of flowering plants in the middle of winter. "That's what I plan to do," he'd noted. "Bloom in a time and place where others are dormant."

What he didn't sketch or comment on in his notes was the little bookstore near Memorial Plaza he'd stepped into in search of a special present for Catherine Rogers. He had worked extra hours at Hedd's after Christmas completing the end-of-the-year inventory, and those earnings were added to what he had already saved for the special trip. He looked for a copy of James Hornell's *String Figures from Fiji and Western Polynesia*. Hornell, a famous zoologist and ethnographer of maritime life, was meticulous in his observation, measurement, and drawing.

By a stroke of good fortune, Oscar found a copy (the storeowner, it turned out, was enamored of string figures), though he paid more than he should for it. While he was waiting to make his purchase, he was distracted by a woman he found strikingly beautiful. On a vacation trip from the East, she appeared older and more sophisticated than he--perhaps a college student or even graduate. She was browsing a Mark Twain display.

Made bold perhaps by being away from home and wanting to be an actor in this new context, Oscar stepped over to explain that what she was viewing was a periodical essay on the Missouri writer's "Platonic Sweetheart," a dream vision that haunted Twain from the time he was Oscar's present age to his death.

Before he knew it, Oscar had invited this stranger to go with him to the site of the 1904 World Fair, which had been hosted by St. Louis. She declined, but graciously, so graciously that she lingered in Oscar's memory.

On the train back to Jefferson City, he felt he'd encountered a vision equal to Samuel Clemens' Platonic Sweetheart. He would never see her again, he was sure. But that didn't mean he couldn't include the memory of her face among the images of beauty that inspired him to pursue lofty goals. He never dreamt how much more she would do for him.

"You see?" Oscar asked Bob. "It's like Frank Lloyd Wright's Wingspread, but the underlying shape is more a rocket than an airplane. It all reaches toward the sky."

"Ah." Bob knew his friend was fascinated by airborne machines, both the engine-less glider cranky Professor Leicht had taken Oscar up in the previous summer and the latest sophisticated rocket-assisted aircraft. Bob knew nothing about the famous architect's house in Wisconsin. "It looks as much like a grain elevator to me."

"Ah, you have no imagination." In the clean lines he'd learned to use in his mechanical drawing class, Oscar saw comfortable, high-ceilinged living spaces, quiet but well lit corners for privacy, expansive views over the surrounding countryside. This would be the home of a man who, having won fame and fortune, was now able to engage the world on his own terms.

"Huh. It's a big house, all right; but it's still just a house."

Oscar was not surprised at his friend's reaction. He felt Bob, studying to become an accountant, had little appreciation for beauty, grandeur, the finer things. Oscar liked to think of himself as a Renaissance man, talented in a variety of academic areas, besides his major of mathematics. He felt he was more open to the world's richness.

Bob shrugged. "Too many years tending goats have made me--unlike your hero Flash Gordon--relentlessly down-to-earth."

"Hmmph. I bet you're down to earth when it comes to pawing Alice." Alice Holder was a day student home economics major at St. Mary's. She'd gone out several times with Bob.

Oscar knew the movie hero was a creature of fantasy, but he did at times imagine himself manning a space ship and defeating Azura, Queen of Mars, and Ming the Merciless.

Bob ignored Oscar's comment. "I read recently that whoever perfects explosive carrying rockets will win the war in Europe. I'm counting on bombers to knock out our enemies' factories first." Like many, he had become convinced the country would be drawn into the conflict.

He couldn't have known, of course, about Germany's secret experimental rocket research station at Peenemünde that would in a few short years produce the V-2s, raining fire on London and other European cities as the war accelerated at a devastating pace.

"I'm not interested in overseas events. This is my dream project, and after I finish architecture school, create my own firm, and design buildings around the world, I'll build it for . . . for me and the most beautiful woman in the world." Oscar planned to continue his education at a prestigious Eastern university.

"And that beautiful woman would be . . . Elsa?"

"Actually," Oscar said evasively, "you don't know her."

He was thinking of Janet Middleton, second best (according to Oscar) mathematician at Wesleyan. A tall, fiery redhead, she taunted him whenever she had a better test score and flirted with him when it made him angry. Her attractive lips were always slightly parted, reminding him of Jeanette MacDonald opposite Nelson Eddy in *Sweethearts*.

"Let's play another game," he said to Bob. Folding his drawings and putting them back in his satchel, he picked up his ping pong paddle, which had a custom made, extra long handle.

This spring Oscar had become obsessed with table tennis. He'd picked up the game at the Y, where high school and college students congregated. His father built a half-table against a side wall he could practice on in the garage. He played himself by banging the ball over a painted net and pretending the rebound came from his imaginary opponent. He got to be very good, but never as good as his friend and rival, Lee.

Two things intrigued Oscar about ping-pong: the competition of speed, timing, and power; and the audience of girls who often watched the boys play. They included Alice, Betty, and--perhaps prettiest of all--his cousin Elsa.

While Elsa continued to be Professor Lewis' star piano student, her family did not have enough money to send her to college. Her three brothers were the family's priority; she would marry, of course, and be provided for in that way. Their hope was that she would play the organ at their church when the current music director stepped down. Oscar saw her only once during the week and on occasional weekends when he traveled with his father to Assyria.

He had finally discovered Elsa's beauty. She'd had a teenage crush on him a few years back, and had since bloomed into a willowy young woman. Oscar's classmates envied him when he met her in the music building and walked her to the mill, where she would ride home with her father. Allowing them to think he and she were a couple was flattering.

Her family liked Oscar, of course, and may well have entertained the idea that the two might one day be more than distant cousins. He toyed with the idea himself, but believed his genius would carry him far away from this country girl. And his mother, wanting him to be 100% American, would oppose a deeper connection to the local Swedish community.

"Well, whoever your dream woman is," Bob said as the ball ricocheted off his paddle, "ask her to the spring formal at St. Mary's."

"I'm planning to be there. But you know I have to perform part of the time." With Larry Wharton (piano) and Mark Strand (drums), he had started up a jazz trio that played at local events. "Besides," he grinned, "I have soooo many choices . . . "

He may not have had many choices, but he did have many hopes. Betty Devine still worked at Hedd's, and he was not immune to her charms. Ever since she'd shown him the painting she did for her parents one Christmas, he was conscious of her nice build--sometimes embarrassingly so. Betty had pictured a manger scene in which the Madonna (unconsciously?) resembled herself and lacked the angelic qualities of traditional representations. But Oscar couldn't get past the real girl's religious intensity, reinforced by her attendance at St. Mary's.

Recently, though, it seemed that she was finding extra ways to be in Oscar's company at places besides Hedd's. She often came to the Y with Lee's sister to play cards and watch the boys at table tennis. And she rooted Oscar on in his epic contests with Lee.

The Shi family had come to Salinas at the same time Oscar started college. According to Bob, who seemed to know these things, they had worked in a Wichita restaurant run by Lee's uncle. Now Lee's parents had established their own business in a new town, even though the social climate was not encouraging to immigrants from Asia.

"People here can't tell the difference between Chinese and Japanese," explained Bob, believing they had no trouble distinguishing Swedish from Norwegian from Dutch from German. "So, a lot of people are suspicious." The first English version of Lee's name was Shi Li Sheng.

Oscar didn't question that local prejudice against Asians, and, like most, he had paid little attention to the details of the ongoing Sino-Japanese conflict pitting one ethnic identity against another. He accepted Lee as worthy table tennis opponent, though he would have grinned without embarrassment at the repeated male joke of those days about any "Oriental" woman's anatomy--not only her eyes were slanted.

It might have been fair to say Oscar's latest heartthrob was more etherial than the slender form of his cousin, the striking beauty of Betty seen in her own painting, the taunting character of Janet, or the mysterious feminine nature of Lee's older sister. Oscar was enamored of a vision he'd encountered when soaring over wheat fields with Professor Leicht. In the light filtering through clouds he'd seen--or so he believed--the face of an angel.

He was well aware that there were scientific explanations for such a sight--electromagnetic fields, lenticular clouds, various kinds of light refraction. And he couldn't discount his own adrenalin-boosted excitement, which might have caused him to distort what he was seeing. Still, even after he had reviewed carefully the entire experience, he remained convinced that what he saw was the image of his beloved waiting for him in some glorious future.

The heady conviction of his destiny inspired by that experience two thousand feet over the ground, however, was chastened before the conclusion of his flight. Moments after the exhilaration of bursting through clouds into almost blinding light, Oscar felt panic as the plane plummeted toward a patch of ground occupied by a small herd of goats. Excited in looking upward, he had not noticed his pilot deliberately taking a nose dive, his favorite maneuver.

They did not crash, catching in time the thermal uplift Professor Leicht knew would be there. Restoring stable flight, the pilot glided safely back to his landing place. But the mental picture Oscar retained from that brief experience came to seem a forewarning of what happened to his friend, Dr. Harold Lewis. And that sad, real event shaped the path he would take into the Second World War.

In his book of drawings that included Wingspread and his own creation, Musica Universalis, Oscar kept one design hidden. Folded in fourths and slipped into the back cover through a slit on the inside were the construction plans for a rocket-assisted sail-plane labeled "PowerPlane." He knew his mother would be opposed to his building anything like such a machine and so kept the idea a secret from all but his friend Bob.

Bob told him he was crazy to want to leave terra firma, and Oscar had received a hint that his father could be as strong as his mother in objecting to experiments in flight. "You know, Oscar," Carl said one day. He had come out to the garage where his son was practicing saxophone solos for his jazz combo. "I owned a motorcycle for one day."

"One day?"

"Ja, one day. Before your mother and I met, I was doing very well. I had a small company building barns for farmers in the county. I had been in Missouri about a year and thought I would have some fun."

Oscar had a hard time picturing his father needing or desiring entertainment. Other than visits to his relatives in Assyria, work occupied all his time. Right now, besides his job as sawyer at

Benson's, he was building cabinets, chairs, and small tables whenever he could get clients.

"Motorcycles can be exciting."

"That is what I thought, so I bought an Indian, bright red, brand new, very powerful." Oscar had been attracted to that brand, often featured in trade magazines, and sometimes idled time away calculating how increased power could be generated by engine modifications.

"I hope you never told Mother about it. She would be scolding you still!"

Carl smiled, a silent laugh. "I have not spoken of it. The fact is that I returned the bike the day after I bought it."

"It was defective?"

"No. It ran very well. But the only riding I had done was on a bicycle. And that was on flat land. The motorcycle was in Jefferson City, with its steep hills and roads winding."

"Ah."

"Ja, the thing took me into a turn so strong the front tire went right out from under me. I was lucky to survive, and I got a bad burn on this leg." He gestured at his left thigh. "There is a nasty scar down my leg, here, from top to the knee."

"Mother's never asked you about it?"

"I tell her that was from my childhood, falling off a sled riding with my brothers. She likes to blame them for it, and I do not mind; so that is what we say."

Oscar nodded his approval of this deception and turned the pages of his music to "Indian Love Call," assuming the chat--a lengthy one for his father--was over. But Carl pointed to the saxophone. "Your music, now. That will not lead you to be hurt like a motorcycle or something with a powerful engine. You keep playing that horn."

As his father turned to go into the house, Oscar studied his back. Could he know about PowerPlane? Well, the project was more a fantasy than a reality, anyway, at least for now; and Oscar soon lost himself in the scene from Rose-Marie where the heroine hums the melody of "Indian Love Call" in her tent, and Sergeant Bruce responds from a lakeside campfire. He wondered what forbidden lover waited for his call, also inspired by an attraction as strong as Romeo and Juliet's? Could it be Janet Middleton? The idea was alluring, if a bit scary.

While she had not grabbed him by his crotch, the Wesleyan co-ed might have been Babs McCauley's or Catherine Roger's successor in Oscar's love life. When, in advanced physics lab, she backed into him, he felt she had done so deliberately. He had turned around just when she was stepping back.

"Is that a pistol in your pocket, or are you just happy to see me?" she asked, smiling over her shoulder and keeping the contact of hip with groin. They were between lab tables on which steel balls, pendulums, and cork guns were assembled.

"No . . . uh, I mean . . . there's nothing . . . "

"Relax, honey. I was just making room here. Pardon the bump."

Oscar reddened and turned back to the ballistic pendulum experiment. He was intensely aware that not only had she echoed Mae West's famous saying, she had used the same husky voice. And she called him "honey"! The image of her tight skirt--which revealed she could apply force to set objects in motion--had burned itself into his brain.

From that meeting early in the spring semester, he had toyed with idea of asking her out. He thought she would be eager for attention because, like him, she had moved a number of times in her past. But the only daughter of an Army colonel, who was retiring to his native state, she had learned to adapt from early childhood. So he held back until a second incident of physical contact seemed to suggest she was potentially interested.

He was uncertain how to interpret her action, so he tried to sound out Bob. "Let me ask you something," he said a few days after Bob had encouraged him to find a date for the spring dance. "Suppose a girl--now, I'm talking about a looker, with a good build . . . suppose she

165

challenges someone to a high jump contest. What should you do? Women can't compete with men in events like that."

"Someone has dared you to beat her?"

"No, this is hypothetical . . . probably. I mean, there is a girl who . . . well, I know she plays tennis and things. And it just occurred to me to wonder . . . "

"I think you politely decline. Be the gentleman."

"That's what I was thinking. But you know, today's women are doing so many things. There's Amelia Earhart. Before her plane disappeared, she had set all sorts of records. Flying requires lots of strength and skill. Well, nerves, too, as much as men."

"Still, you don't go head-to-head with them. We're different beings. I don't think any girl would challenge you to a contest with PowerPlane!"

But Janet had challenged him to a high jump competition, maybe because she was interested in him in some way. The topic had come up in another physic lab, this one about propulsion.

The goal was to send a balloon-powered wooden car up a ramp with a long straight stretch gradually curving into a rise. At the top, the car had to jump a gap and descend, circling back to the starting point. Calculating how much force was needed to maintain speed on the uphill ramp and across the gap was the challenge. Too little and the car stalled or fell into the gap; too much and it could slip off the ramp at either the first or the second curve.

"Hmm," Oscar proposed to Janet, his partner in the experiment. "We could inflate the balloon, measure the circumference, set the car on the track, and record the effects. Increasing it each time, we'll arrive at the proper formula. We''ll have to hope the balloon doesn't stretch as we go."

"But I am going to get tired blowing it up a hundred times."

"We could alternate." He raised his eyebrows. "But why you, anyway?"

She cocked her head at him. "I think it would be better if one did it--we each keep our spit to ourselves." She grinned. "I've run track, you know, and have pretty good wind." She breathed deeply, expanding her chest. Oscar took note.

But he also thought of Babe Didrikson, recently married to George Zaharias and famous for all sorts of athletic accomplishments. Because she was from a Scandinavian family, his Swedish relatives often referred to her achievements.

"Well, I do play the saxophone. That takes lung power, too."

"That's done sitting down. It's better to have the whole body involved. Take the high jump, my speciality--training involves exercises for the arms, chest, the back."

He was about to remind her that he marched in parades while playing. And, although he might not be John Carter of Mars, he was a good jumper.

"Men . . . " He paused, not wanting to offend her, even though he was assuming his sex was superior. "Men can high jump, too."

"Is that so? How about we have a friendly contest, just the two of us."

"I don't see why not. I'll spot you . . . ah, three inches. After lab next week?"

"Deal! But I won't need the spot."

As he turned back to their lab table, Oscar felt her step up close to his side and heard her whisper, "You're going to need a boost, mister." He jumped when she pinched his behind.

Chapter Twenty-three: Descent

At times that spring Oscar felt a good angel was whispering in one ear and a bad angel in the other, except that neither Professor Bohns (mathematics) nor Professor Faire (English literature) was evil. But each wanted him to pursue graduate work in his or her field; and he felt the appeal of both disciplines.

"To study mathematics," argued Dr. Bohns, "is to explore the very structure of all human understanding--relationship, degree, extent. It gives order to the sciences, to philosophy and the languages, to the essence of history. And you have a gift, Mr. Lindbloom. Do not reject your calling." Oscar had won the coveted sophomore prize for mathematics by solving three calculus problems in under an hour.

Dr. Bohns had gotten his graduate degrees at the University of Chicago, published some fine papers on esoteric geometric concepts, and retreated to an endowed chair at his alma mater. He was so tall and thin, some students joked that, like Toto, he would be blown from Kansas to the land of Oz (where many thought he belonged).

Miss Faire was a match in physical build, if not as tall as her colleague. And she seemed as little able to keep her hold on earth as her counterpart except for the ferocious energy she brought to the appreciation of Shakespeare.

"Oscar," she told him, "you have the soul of a poet and a command of language that belongs to the ages. It might be drama, epic poetry, or the serial novel of Dickens and his contemporaries, but your voice must be your vocation." She nominated his essay on "Shakespeare's 'Eye of Heaven'" for a national competition.

He had not told either that his dream was to be an architect and create structures that reached toward heaven. And if that goal proved out of reach (so to speak), he believed he would always have music to travel the realm of human emotion. He did wish Professor Lewis--now as much a friend as a teacher--would free himself from his obsession with the world of politics and devote more time to directing Oscar in his understanding of music.

"Czechoslovakia is gone," he had told Oscar recently at The Ivory Tower, the college's coffee shop. "The deal in Munich is just what we thought--a complete disaster."

"I heard about it on the radio--Bohemia and Moravia become a protectorate. But that's what they've always done in the Old World, invade, be invaded, invade back. Thirty year wars, hundred year wars--it's why so many writers and scientists have come to America. It's not always religious freedom, as you've taught me, but artistic and academic opportunity, too."

"Yes, those who could get away. You remember Mrs. Balogh?"

170

Oscar covered his cup with his hand to stop the waitress from refilling it. "Band director, sure. She went back home the last year I was at the high school. We never knew why, though didn't she have a husband back in her country?"

Her departure had come soon after the spring band trip, where Salinas distinguished itself by the performance of a new composition by Mrs. Balogh's countryman. The event was written up in the Kansas City papers, drawing attention to the groundbreaking nature of the piece.

Oscar recalled the trip fondly because his friend Bob ecstatically recorded his first kiss (surely, kisses) on that excursion, and he himself had a clandestine reunion with Catherine Rogers. In a school closet they revisited the roles of nurse and patient, reversing them and assessing her reflexes. He struck her knee lightly with his timpani hammer and then worked his way up via a series of taps and jerks, generating higher and higher tones, as if she were a saxophone and his hammer fingers.

Professor Lewis explained. "Mrs. Balogh was married to a Jew. He went into hiding because he couldn't get permission to leave their country; but he insisted she come here. There was a hope that he could be smuggled out of his country to Sweden and eventually find a way to rejoin her. But . . . "

"But . . . ?"

He shook his head and, seeing the waitress approach, pointed at his coffee cup. Oscar drank his coffee black, copying his father, who explained that adding cream and sugar was not something Swedish men did. Professor Lewis' coffee was caramel colored.

"I really don't know. She received a letter from the authorities that he was to be tried for unspecified 'crimes against the state' unless she returned to testify in his behalf. We didn't believe it was anything more than a way of forcing her to return. But she couldn't stay here believing he was in custody."

"And you never learned what happened?"

"There are many cases like this. The people just . . . they just disappear."

Oscar pictured Superman escaping his enemies with a single bound over a tall building and then returning to pulverize them all. He didn't know what to say about what had happened to the band director. "Mr. Hedd has been talking about this, too, at the shoe store. I hope he doesn't have relatives back there. He's lived his whole life in Salinas, or at least I think he has." He knew that his boss received a lot of mail from overseas, but he always assumed they involved business.

"Oscar, we may not have relatives or even friends in Europe, but what happens over there affects us over here. We have to hope that England, France, and the other free countries wake up in time to stop Hitler. You'd think we'd all learned from the war in Spain!"

Oscar assented quietly and explained that he had to leave now for physics lab. "I'll come back, soon, though. You make me think about issues I have a tendency to ignore."

"I'd like to pretend we live in Valhalla as well, our involvement in conflict over; but I'm afraid that's not going to be possible."

Oscar chuckled at his friend's reference to Norse mythology. Professor Lewis had been studying Wagner's *Ring of the Niebelungen* and occasionally asked Oscar about such famous Scandinavian works as *The Poetic Etta* and the *Volsunga Saga*. While Oscar's encyclopedic knowledge included many of those myths, the only striking image he retained was of the cosmic ash tree, Yggdrasill.

He connected the idea of universe built into a tree with the Renaissance Great Chain of Being, hierarchical structures rising up out of the chaos of lesser worlds. Music continued to offer a means of ascent, or at least a temporary escape from lowly existence.

Because Valhalla was the celestial home of warriors, Oscar was reminded of his Uncle John, who was in danger of losing his earthly residence. Oscar's mother had received a letter from Agnes explaining that she might have to move her husband to the Old Soldiers' Home in St. James. She had exhausted her savings and, as his sickness worsened and he needed more care, she was having trouble keeping her cafe operating.

"That's an hour south of Jefferson City at least," she told Oscar. "He'll die there in less than a year without her."

"Does that mean she has to pay to keep him there?"

"From what I understand, no. But the Home's staff decide what treatment he receives, what he is given to eat, even what he can wear. It's . . . it's a fall for a family."

No one in Sallie's family had ever had to get help from the state, though in times of emergency neighbors and church members routinely brought food, assisted with chores, and sat with the sick. Those in the community who faced failure moved west down Route 66 rather than accept the banks' label of bankruptcy.

Oscar knew that his mother's unyielding work ethic came from the pioneer spirit of her ancestors. And Carl--who'd come to this country with a Bible, a Swedish-English dictionary, and the clothes on his back--had kept them solvent for a decade of hard times, tirelessly applying himself to menial labor. They were committed to their son's attending college, going on to professional school, and moving in circles to which they had never aspired.

Despite the fact that the possibility of a collapse was always just beneath the surface of family life, when Oscar read *The Grapes of Wrath*, he automatically connected himself and his parents with the hardy survivors. Since the dark days of 1929, his parents had moved on when necessary, started over, made their way. They would continue to do so.

Of course, he also daydreamed about the people in Steinbeck's novel, as he did with many of the movies he saw and books he read. The character of Rose of Sharon intrigued him, because, she was both pure and pregnant. Still, Muley's characterization of himself, "jerkin' like a billy goat under a bush in the night,'" appealed to another side of Oscar's longing.

Chapter Twenty-four: Steps

"One-two-three, one-two-three." Miss Young was directing her dance students and making Oscar's head hurt. Two nights a week he picked up much-needed extra money accompanying the six to ten young girls at Salinas' own High Pointe Dance Studio.

This ancient lady claimed to have danced in Argentina, Hong Kong, Las Vegas, and the French Riviera. But her palm thumping on her desk, precise though its rhythm was, and the inept landings of her hapless pupils in front of him, were pounding Oscar's brain into the dust.

The teacher held up a hand to stop the music, "To the bar, ladies. You are so listless that you must watch yourself in the mirror for a time. Mr. Lindbloom will continue to play."

She gestured to him and disappeared into what she called her "office," a corner blocked off by folding bamboo panels. Oscar was pretty sure she kept a flask of something that lifted her spirits (so to speak) in the drawer of that little desk.

The only bright spot in these three-hour sessions for him was the chance to visit with Lee's sister, Beth. (When she first came to town, she called herself "Shi Bai Tiao," but, like her brother, finally allowed the romanization in order to make English speakers comfortable.) Something in her sad eyes and quiet ways made him feel she had a story to tell, one of suffering, ennui, heartbreak. And that appealed to his thirst for exotic experience.

He had been in the studio when Beth first approached Miss Young without a resume, but demonstrating remarkable skills.

"Where did you study, my child? You have the steps of someone with great training."

"It does not matter," she explained. "It was with my aunt in . . . in Wichita. She trained in our country before she came here."

"Well, if you accept the terms I'm offering, you will please me as my assistant. Two nights each week and all day Saturdays."

No one was quite sure of Miss Young's nationality, though many believed her small stature and dark hair meant she was "Oriental," at least in part. She had been in Salinas for twenty years, did not travel, and (according to the post office gossip) received no mail. Still, she provided a service townspeople found worthwhile.

Oscar asked her assistant at a pause between numbers, "Beth, will you be coming to the Y tomorrow? I'm hoping Lee will be there so I can drub him at table tennis."

She gave only the faintest of smiles at his joke (if anyone would be beaten soundly, it was Oscar). "I do not know yet. I must work at the Red Dragon through lunch and again at dinner. Perhaps there will be time."

The family restaurant stood out in Salinas' downtown, with its miniature version of Los Angeles' East Gate on Broadway. The triple roofs with sweeping corners and bright colors seemed out of place amid the conventional square brick buildings, but the Red Dragon was well run, inexpensive, and comfortable. Its lines impressed Oscar, though its horizontal reach was counter to the upward movement he preferred.

"You need a break," Oscar asserted. "Too many more pas de cheval and you're going to have to find a horse and ride out of here."

Again, this won him only a slight grin. "I do not mind. These girls are only doing what their parents want them to. And that is a good lesson to learn."

Oscar was not ready to agree to that, but he knew better than to press the point. Instead, he asked, wanting as much as anything else to prolong the conversation, "I was wondering . . . you've watched me play ping-pong, and you know Lee's game, would you have any tips for me? I mean I'd like to get better because that will help him get better."

Once more she smiled and ducked her head. "Forgive me, but perhaps you go for the big shot too often. It's not how many flashy hits one makes but how many points are scored."

He knew she was right. He had worked hard to develop both a backhand and forehand smash, but sometimes lost concentration dwelling on the rush of a previous shot's success. Good at many things, he did not like to practice and felt strategy was beneath a man of his talent. But today he worried that losing badly to Lee might affect his confidence in the high jump contest later. So he did take Beth's advice and tried to play more deliberately. It seemed to pay off.

Lee had been at the challenge table for over an hour when Oscar arrived. The main hall of the center contained two more ping pong tables, four pool tables, and a row of pinball machines along one wall. A snack bar was next door where card players congregated.

In a system as old as the center, whoever won the present game took on the challenger. Players put themselves forward by sticking a card with a name on it under the top frame of a bulletin board. The custom governed play on the challenge billiards table also. On busy days, a dozen cards could be posted for each game. And good players often stayed at play for hours.

Betty was among those watching, and Oscar anticipated her encouragement when his turn arrived. He and she were always comfortable together, having worked side-by-side so many years at Hedd's. Long tenure there had earned them privileges, like being left alone to staff the store on Saturdays. So, as they worked they shared a lot of their triumphs and failures at school.

"What did your art professor say about your new piece?" he asked her as he was waiting for Lee to dispatch his current opponent. Oscar knew she had worked a long time on a painting of Elijah being transported by a whirlwind to heaven.

"I think he liked it, but he wanted to know what happened to the chariot of fire. 'Wasn't that part of the story?' he asked."

Oscar nodded. "No matter what you do, they always want you to do something more, or even something different." He knew more about Elijah from having read the encyclopedia than from attending Sunday school. But he discounted the whole idea of leaders chosen by God--individuals controlled history by their will and abilities, he believed.

"I asked Reverend James about Elijah." Betty frowned. "And he said there are different interpretations of that passage. Some think the prophet flew up in the whirlwind, and that the chariots are just part of the background. Others believe that horses and chariot are necessary for Elijah to be carried away. Myself, I was intrigued by the challenge of picturing a whirlwind--I mean, it's really just air, isn't it?"

"Right. Its shape is only seen by what it drives along. Now, me, if I thought people were being lifted off the earth and carried away today, I'd conclude we're being visited by beings from outer space."

Oscar had continued to include science fiction in his recreational reading at college, even re-reading Edgar Rice Burroughs' Martian books from time to time. Though he was taking a full load at Wesleyan and working two jobs, he still had time to drift away into other worlds. When he listened to Orson Welles' famous broadcast of *The War of the Worlds*, he become excited, not afraid. For a few hours he believed the time had come for heroic acts of courage and bold strokes of genius.

"We'd need God to look after us even more if space ships were on the way to earth." She frowned. "Unless, of course, they were a plague that came upon us for our sins."

"I don't think aliens are coming anywhere except to the movies. By the way, do you know what will be on next week at the Orpheum?"

He was hoping to change the topic, though he had to admit his penchant for stories of other worlds and Betty's belief in a life after death were not altogether dissimilar. But you didn't have to give up pleasure to enter his realm of fantasy. And Oscar knew that anyone who hoped to enjoy Betty's beauty in this life would have to do so within the bounds of holy matrimony.

He would later see that one of his favorite science fiction movies, *Things to Come*, was eerily prophetic, as Elijah's words were supposed to be, according to the Bible. The futuristic movie starring Raymond Massey predicted the rise of despotic tyrants, a global conflict, and reaction against the destructive nature of science in war. That part of the plot was farfetched to Oscar, but the idea that someone might invent and pilot a rocket to reach the moon struck him as a believable scenario.

When the match with Lee got under way, he was pleased to see Elsa visiting with Betty. Betty sang in her church choir, so the two had much in common. But Oscar assumed they were both enjoying his skilled performance.

Was there any chance Janet might be looking on, also? He scanned the room, but didn't see her face in the crowd. He did, however, spot someone he knew: Mark "Tank" Thompson was intently studying his battle with Lee.

Chapter Twenty-five: Lobs

Oscar's win against Lee that day was a surprise. While he had to credit his more careful play, Lee also seemed to miss more shots than usual; and he left with Beth after that game. Perhaps family matters were distracting him.

Next up at the challenge table to meet Oscar? Tank, the giant.

Oscar hadn't seen his former rival for some months. Bigger (or at least wider) and stronger than ever, the former high school star was now playing football at the University of Kansas. Tank returned home occasionally, where he was publicly touted by civic leaders and privately worshiped by young athletes.

He and Oscar had never had occasion to clash after the big man lifted the daydreamer out of the way of a rattling Model A Ford on the day of the homecoming parade. Oscar left high school at the end of that year, and they had moved in different circles thereafter.

In that earlier time, Diana Light thought she had achieved her goal of claiming the town star, but Tank, courted by several universities over the next few months, came to realize there were many more attractive women eager to walk with an arm in his. Not to be pitied, Diana told him she no longer wished him to call and convinced her parents to send her with her white gloves to a private finishing school in Virginia.

"I was watching you, Squarehead," Tank told Oscar as he came up to the table tennis table. "You're pretty good."

"Oh, that game was luck. Lee is the best around here. Well, at least until you showed up." Oscar saw no reason not to try flattery to soften the tone of the coming contest. "Shall we lob for serve?"

Local rules called for both players to hit a ball over the net as close to the far edge as possible without missing it. Good players could often have the ball nick the edge, barely changing the arc of its flight. Whoever won the lob could either choose to serve first or to stand at a particular end, perhaps feeling the light was better there.

Oscar didn't like the practice, which he saw as too imprecise. Sometimes it was difficult to judge the spot of impact; and now and then a player would fudge the mark. But the custom was well established, and to question it would make him look as if he doubted his ability.

"So, how's the team shaping up for next year?" Oscar asked after his lob, not wanting to seem focused only on winning.

"We'll be strong." Tank took his lob, which bettered Oscar's. "I guess you're the number one student in your college class?"

"Oh, that's hard to say." Oscar, in fact, had made straight A's throughout. "But I'm doing all right."

Tank chose to serve first, and Oscar took the side by the windows, the light behind him. He was surprised at Tank's quickness and the comfortable way he played the game. But then, thought Oscar, natural athletes are good at all sports. Tank must have also faced his fellow university athletes in all sorts of competition.

What puzzled Oscar was why Tank had seemed intent on engaging him at all. The growing circle of spectators, most of them girls, made Oscar think he didn't need this small stage to get attention. Tank played in front of thousands in Lawrence.

"I read that you switched to fullback," Oscar observed. Actually, Bob had told him. "I guess the runners get more of the spotlight?"

"Ah, it wasn't my choice. I'm low to the ground and strong, so defensive players have a hard time ganging up on me. I meet 'em one at a time, and they . . . well, they tend to go backwards when I go forwards."

"I see. Now that I think about it, I'm pretty sure I wouldn't want to see your helmet coming straight at me."

"No worry about our butting heads in an unfriendly way. And I don't want to have to match wits with you on a calculus exam."

Oscar found that his opponent played a close game, aiming short, angled shots just over the net, rather than a power game, which involved standing back from the table and blasting drives. Oscar was having little chance to finish points with his own smashes.

He also saw that Elsa and Betty were now watching the game. Their attention, in addition to the unexpectedly conversational Tank, made it difficult for him to concentrate. In some ways he was ready to relinquish the challenge table, as his main goal had been to record a win against Lee. Yet his competitive nature made it hard to give up, especially against an old rival.

"Say, Oscar, you seemed to know that guy who just played--'Lee,' did you say?"

"Right. His family started up the Red Dragon, center of town. When was that? Maybe three years ago."

Oscar worried that Tank was going to object to a Chinese guy at the Y. The big man had resented immigrants from Europe, who at least looked (to him) like regular Kansas residents. What did he think about Orientals?

"That's a pretty nice restaurant. Rotary had a dinner there in the fall, and I was asked to . . . to ah, make a few remarks."

"It's good food. I hope their meal was enough for you!"

186

He was alluding to the popular idea that you're hungry an hour after you eat Chinese food. He himself never felt that way because he followed the advice of his father, who'd known what it was not to have enough to eat. He always told him he should always push away from the table just a little bit hungry.

At the ping pong table, Oscar found himself on the defensive, forced to adjust his game to Tank's. He needed to take some shots earlier instead of being kept back on his heels.

Carl's Spartan diet, of course, sometimes angered Sallie, who'd grown up cooking in a farm kitchen, where the men needed that full breakfast of eggs, meat, biscuits and gravy to work in the field all day. While she couldn't afford expensive cuts these days, she still tended to prepare more than her men would eat.

"Ha-ha," said Tank. "The Chinese know that's what we think about their food! Probably why they bought me two dishes. But the coaches say I'm supposed to fill up because the guys I'm going against are loading it on as much as they can, too."

Conventional wisdom also held that, because the Asian physique was small, slender, strong, they were excellent table tennis players. He connected Lee's ability with Beth's skill in dance. And, because they were both reserved, they also fit the stereotype of inscrutability.

Oscar realized that classifying people in this way sometimes created ironies. The Charlie Chan character in the popular movie series was played by American actors, who possessed a star power it was assumed could never be earned by a person of another race. It didn't seem to occur to many that the actor's pretending to be Oriental could involve an erosion of his mainstream identity.

Warner Orland, a Swede, first played Chan. He'd died recently, though, and Sidney Toler had taken his place. Before he passed away, Orland was being filmed in *Charlie Chan at the Ringside*. The story was rewritten to fit another series about an Asian detective, *Mr. Moto's Gamble*. In that film Austrian-American (and Jewish) actor Peter Lorre depicts Moto, this time attending a boxing match when he becomes caught up in a murder investigation.

"My ad," announced Tank.

Oscar had felt his energy sag. While playing, he had let his thoughts wander to a movie scene in which a scantily clad girl in a boxing ring held up a sign with the number of the round on it. Then he pictured Beth's slim figure before the mirror in her ballet shoes. And there was Janet in some sort of track suit springing toward the high jump bar.

He scanned the now sizable crowd, who were, from time to time, politely applauded the play. Concern was visible on Betty's face. And

Elsa didn't seem to be able to watch anymore. He needed to pull himself together and rally.

"Deuce," admitted Tank after Oscar set up a successful backhand smash. This was more like it!

Elsa was whispering something to Betty, who frowned. She then whispered back to Elsa, while still watching Oscar and Tank. Elsa nodded. Must be the usual gossip girls indulge in, Oscar concluded, and returned to the game.

Rather than a seeing a white ball tossed up in front of a ping pong paddle, Oscar envisioned Mrs. Balogh holding a letter up in front of her and slapping it with her other hand; and he heard his cousin Elsa telling Professor Lewis about Jews trying to escape to Sweden. He lost the game.

Oscar's lapses in concentration cost him the match with Tank. A similar loss of focus affected his performance against Janet. But this time it was not what he pictured in his mind that weakened his effort, but what he saw in the flesh--literally, thanks to Janet's revealing sporting outfit. The experience did, however, stoke his desire to take her to the dance at St. Mary's.

Approaching the weekend, it occurred to Oscar that, despite all the fences he'd sailed over and the creeks he'd vaulted, he really didn't know anything about how to compete in a track event. So, at the Wesleyan library he read up on the traditional scissors-kick style, in which the jumper leads with one leg as a hurdler might, then pulls the trail leg up and over as he clears the pole. The body stays upright.

But he also learned that some jumpers have more success with the "western roll." Here the jumper approaches the bar more from the side, kicking over with the lead leg and letting the body roll across the bar horizontally. Babe Didrikson had shocked a lot of people when she adopted this style for the 1932 Olympics, which some officials insisted was not technically a "jump." Oscar decided he would try both methods.

"You're not going to clear our goat fence," Bob insisted, gesturing at the wire structure. "And if you come flying in there, they're going to think you're food."

"Hmph. I could clear your fence easily, but what I want you to do is hold this pole at the end and put the other end here." He pointed to the five-foot mark on a tape measure he had hung from a nail in the fence's corner post. "We'll raise it two inches each time."

"Okay, but I think you should be spending more time practicing your dance steps than high jumping. Have you asked your dream girl to trip the light fantastic yet?"

"Not yet." Oscar hoped that next week's contest would provide just that opportunity.

"Well, you'd better get busy. Remember, you can ride with us." Bob was allowed to drive his father's car on important occasions. "And you'll feel bad watching Alice and me do the St. Louis Shag while you're stuck on your band stool."

Oscar was surprised. That dance had a number of lively steps, including the "stag" (lifting the leg with the knee bent); and some couples would add two kicks, switching feet rather than rocking on them. His friend must have been working on the moves!

"Well, it is tricky for me because my date would have to sit out when I'm playing."

"At least you get to come free. Anyway, Alice's looking forward to hearing your group. Have you settled on a name yet?"

"'Prairie Heaven.' We're getting pretty good, too."

The name had come to him after his glider flight. The sky in Kansas always seems enormous, with nothing breaking the view across the plains. But in flight it was as if he were approaching a union of land and air at the horizon--heaven. When he played Bing Cosby's "Pennies from Heaven," in which "each cloud contains" a fortune, he recalled this experience.

"Hold it there," he told Bob and then, using the western roll, cleared his first mark.

"You know," Bob observed, "you haven't actually told me that you have someone to jump against, girl or boy." He put the bar up another two inches.

"This is just an experiment. One day I might need to know how to do this." He got over that level, though he could tell it was close.

"You're going to hurt yourself if you try much higher."

"Go up two inches. If I make that, no girl . . . uh, no one is going to beat me."

This time his shirt, loose at the belly, touched the pole; so he was approaching a limit. Still, he was impressed with his own performance.

192

It didn't occur to either of the boys that success doesn't come entirely in the mechanics of jumping. Not only are there exercises to strengthen certain muscles, but the approach can also make a significant difference in the launch itself. And the speed of take-off has to be measured so that momentum goes into upward as well as forward movement.

Nonetheless, Oscar felt confident that he would not be beaten by a girl and that the girl he was jumping against would get an invitation to a dance. Before he made his offer, though, he had to dodge Betty's strong suggestion that he take Beth Shi.

At Hedd's that weekend she was consoling him about his loss to Tank. "It's all right," he explained. " I was . . . thinking of other things. And I'd just beaten Lee, who's really the best around."

"That's true." She paused. She was rearranging the window display and had asked Oscar to bring out the stepladder for her. "They're such a nice family. Have you ever met the parents?"

"No. I really only see Lee at the Y. My parents don't go out to eat very much." In fact, because their budget was tight, they'd not gone out a single time since moving to Salinas.

Betty had stepped up three rungs on the ladder to adjust a female mannikin's hair. The figure (nicknamed "Hetty" Hedd) was positioned on a pedestal so her feet would be closer to eye level for people passing by. As Betty reached up, Oscar noted her full figure in the flowery dress. "I've been to their house," she explained. "Beth has been attending our church from time to time, and she thought my coming over might encourage them to come, too."

Lee had mentioned to Oscar that his family was Christian, converted by Presbyterian missionaries some generations back. "Do they like a different church here?"

"No. I think something happened where they were . . . in Wichita, I guess . . . and they've not been going to any church."

Oscar decided he didn't need to know and didn't want the subject of his own attending to come up. "Wait right there, and I'll step out on the street to tell you how it looks."

Betty stayed on the ladder, and he gave her a thumbs up. She smiled and did a little curtesy, one knee bent, the other foot lifted a bit toward the back. Oscar felt a little rush of appreciation for her coy pose and sweet nature. She was a good friend to have.

When he came around to remove the ladder, Betty said, "That reminds me. Lee's sister, Beth, would kind of like to go the dance at St. Mary's. She could be my guest, but . . . um . . . do you know anyone who might take her?"

"She would be a swell dance partner. Of course, we're not playing any songs for ballet steps. It's all swing."

"She says Lee has taught her all the new steps. And they dance to the radio at night. She'd be a lot of fun . . . for someone."

Oscar felt cornered. He recalled how a moment of pity had led him to invite Betty to the homecoming parade several years ago. "Tell you what," he told her, "there's a nice boy in my physics class, smart and nice looking. Let me talk to him."

Betty smiled her thanks, but he knew it wasn't what she had been hinting. He just hoped she didn't realize he'd made up this available fellow student out of whole cloth. At least he didn't claim the boy had "a great personality."

While Janet did have a great personality, it was something else that riveted his attention the next week as they met to compete. His mouth may even have gaped when, in getting ready for her first attempt, she slipped off a light coat.

"A good jumper needs to keep her legs free, right?" she explained, sweeping a hand below her midsection. "I'd wear a swimsuit, but it's a bit chilly still for that. Still, I can kick in these." She certainly could--a pair of loosely fitting shorts that didn't go an inch down her thighs.

Looking away and nearly blushing, he said, "I wear these slacks for tennis. They're loose enough--slack, ha-ha! So, anyway, how do we do this?" They were on the school's track; the team was away at a match and the field was empty.

"We do it just like the Olympics. We each have three tries to clear a certain height. Then, it goes up an inch. We both keep jumping until one doesn't make it."

"Remember, I said I'd have to go three inches higher."

"And I said I didn't need the spot." She tapped him on the shoulder, and he almost jumped again, remembering her pinching him and saying he was going to need a boost.

"All right, then. Ladies first." He stepped to the end of the bar to make sure it was at the agreed upon height, while she circled back to a starting point.

He was surprised and impressed at her bounding, curving approach, each stride elevating her body vertically like a rocket. Then she came directly at him. When her take-off kick came, he felt she was going to sail over or onto his head. And then, as her foot cleared the bar, he couldn't keep from looking into the widening gap between those shorts and whatever. Did he see red?

He didn't care if he won or lost. "Come with me to the dance at St. Mary's," he blurted. "You'll be the most . . . the best . . . the girl there."

The week before the dance, Oscar began parting his hair in the middle. He had always had thick, dark hair, and brushing back the sides gave him, with his wire-rimmed glasses, a foreign, intellectual look. He hoped it would cause Janet to think of him as more sophisticated than he'd felt when he'd asked her for a date.

"I'd like to go," she'd said smiling. They were resting on the grass beside the track. She'd draped her coat over her shoulders but was still breathing heavily from the series of jumps. "I hear you're the rising jazz star. And maybe some of the other boys there will ask me to dance when you're playing."

"Sure. That would be swell. So long as you go home 'with the guy who brung you.'"

"'Brung' me?"

"It's from a song I heard. It just means you'll be my date, even if . . . "

"No one will steal me. After all, you'll probably the best high jumper there--among the boys, I mean."

He pulled up a few blades of grass and studied them. "I . . . uh . . . guess I should have done a bit more practicing. The way you come up to the bar really helps you elevate."

197

Oscar may, in fact, have jumped higher than Janet, but unfortunately he reached the highest point just before or just after he was at the bar. He hadn't polished the techniques of approach and take-off.

"I had that one lucky jump," she offered graciously. "I probably couldn't do it again." She pointed a finger at him. "But I do win the bet."

"The bet? I'm not sure what we actually wagered."

"Oh, well, I'll remind you at the dance." She rose and shook out her hair. "If you don't misbehave in physics before then!"

"Like getting a better score on the test-- again?" They began walking toward the street.

"Right. But I think that was a fluke. I'll do better on the optics exam."

They passed through the gate in the fence that surrounded the track, so Oscar said, "This is where I have to go to work. But thanks for the lesson in flight. It was fun."

She laughed. "Oh, I'm hoping to rise, all right! And this was quite a workout today!"

She spread her coat to cool off in the breeze. When she lifted her arms, Oscar could see the perspiration stains under her arms. Involuntarily, he glanced at her legs and took a mental picture that was slightly disturbing, though he didn't know why. They glistened with sweat, too.

Before he might make another clumsy comment, he waved and started on his way. The day had been exhilarating, and lyrics to "*Let's Fall in Love*" ran through his head: "Let's close our eyes / And make our own paradise." What, he wondered, would happen at the dance?

Oscar asked the same question a few days later. His mother had asked him to go over to St. Mary's. "Deliver this to Betty Devine for me." She handed him a package, which he assumed to be clothes she had mended for the other family.

"Shouldn't I just drop them by her house? It's not out of the way."

"No, I promised Mrs. Devine I'd get this to her daughter at noon. She says Betty can meet you at the gate."

A man couldn't come on St. Mary's campus unescorted. The girls had to sign out to go anywhere and after dark on weekdays were not allowed to leave with anyone but a parent, though Betty had standing permission to go home and to Hedd's for work. Oscar still thought being a student at this school was like living in a nunnery.

"I guess I can cut short my study time. What is this anyway--clothes?" He hefted the package, guessing the contents by weight.

"Never you mind. Just do as I ask you." Seeing his father's look, he agreed. Ever since his mother's breakdown, he was careful to watch for signals from Carl about her mood and how he should respond.

As promised, Betty was waiting for him at the gate, though she asked him to step into the lobby for a few minutes, "if he had time." He was worried that the subject of a date for Beth would come up again; but, because she was a good friend, he agreed.

She put him at ease immediately. "By the way, that favor I asked, about Beth--you don't need to worry. She received an invitation to the dance and is excited to be going. She and her date will be my guests."

"That's nice. I . . don't think . . . Jeremy . . . was going to be available. Anyway, here's the package my mother sent. I hope it's what you were expecting."

Betty had on a pretty skirt and blouse, again accenting her attractive figure. When she stepped up to take the package, a scent of shampoo or perfume or soap washed over him. He was reminded that when she smiled, which she did just then, she was strikingly pretty.

She folded the package in her arms without examining it. "Thanks. I'm sure this is right. It's . . . ." She paused and looked at him. "I like the way you're wearing your hair now. It's like a movie star." Her gaze made her look to Oscar like a movie star herself, waiting for love.

Betty had a quality he'd recognized for a long time, though it both drew him and pushed him away. Her intensity about the church--about Jesus and salvation--put him off. He couldn't believe himself that questioning was a sin, that doubters would be cast down into the fires of hell forever. But at the same time, her absolute faith in the existence of a higher being gave Betty a fineness that other girls lacked, even girls he found attractive. It would be good in a sister, but not a lover.

He thought of Babs McCauley, his early tutor in the art of erotic contact--not exactly refined. His encounters with Catherine, for whom an eye exam had been an excuse to explore the male body, had been complicated by . . . well, saxophone spit. Janet, whose saucy nature was exciting, lost some of her appeal by being . . . sweaty. Betty's physical charms had a simplicity, a cleanness. Would she . . . could she, he wondered, respond to his . . . well, to a boy's advances?

Because she kept smiling and hugging the package, Oscar felt awkward and asked, "Will I see you at the dance, then?"

"Yes," she said. "Actually, your cousin Henrik is taking me." He was Elsa's brother.

Oscar liked Henrik, though he found him a bit dull. Neither an athlete nor a scholar, he was a hard worker who would probably stay in Assyria and work a portion of his father's land.

"Yes. I've not seen him dance . . . but that's good that you're coming. Um, was there something else I should do for you? Take something back to Mother?"

She looked down and seemed uncertain. She put a hand shyly on his arm. "Oscar, I need to tell you this. Please forgive me, but your mother . . . she thinks we should . . . see each other, I guess. She had you bring this today--it's an old dress she wore once, long ago--just so we would end up in the same place. I'm sorry, and I know this embarrasses you."

He stepped back and looked at the ceiling. "Ah, I see. She's worries about me, I know--wants me to be more . . . settled. But mothers shouldn't be matchmakers in this day and age. Not that you are I are not friends, good friends and . . . well, our fathers work at the same place, so do we. But we have to . . . we have to decide about these sorts of things ourselves."

Despite himself, he heard Eddy Duchin's orchestra, "We might have been meant for each other / To be or not to be, / let our hearts discover."

Betty had been a constant in his life. He'd seen her more regularly than any other girl since coming to Salinas--well, or before. As much as he liked her, he couldn't quite think of her as . . . as the dream girl for whom he'd always waited. But he didn't want to have to tell her that.

Again, she put him at ease. "I agree. We have to choose our own destiny. And I'll tell you a secret, since we have known each other quite

202

some time, and we are . . . good friends. I may have found someone. It's not Henrik, though I'll enjoy going to the dance with him. But the boy I . . . I like is . . . well, not free right now."

Oscar was certain that, in the same way he'd made up "Jeremy," she was making this lover up so he wouldn't feel bad. If there had been someone, she'd have given him hints at work, if not directly by her manner. And because she was coming so often to watch him play ping pong at the Y, he was convinced she hoped, just like his mother, he would one day discover feelings for her. What he needed to do now was accept her little fiction and make her feel comfortable.

"That's wonderful. You . . . deserve to find someone. And I'll keep your secret until . . . until the day he is free."

Impulsively, he gave her a little hug and was again struck by sweet smells. She embraced him in return, but her arms did not hold him. And they parted.

Sitting in the exposed rumble seat of the Petersons' '37 Chevrolet on the evening of the spring dance, Oscar contemplated the distant horizon at twilight. Bob's date lived on the edge of town, and he had parked at the end of her lane. While he was walking up to the Holders' porch to reassure Alice's father that he would be the gentleman this evening, Oscar imagined dancing with Janet into the wee hours--and not being the gentleman.

He and and his attractive date were Fred Astaire and Ginger Rogers effortlessly performing "The Waltz of the Red Balloons" from *Shall We Dance*. That movie's hero wanted to combine ballet with jazz, and Oscar believed he had the musical and physical skills to carry it off--with Janet breathless in his arms, of course.

As his mind pursued the dance sequence, his eyes recorded the shifting lights and colors of a sunset over the plains. Shapes of orange, red, yellow, white, and a fading blue appeared, shifted in form, merged into others. He recalled the face in the clouds he'd seen from Professor Leicht's sailplane, a beauty not associated with anyone he'd ever seen. Or was it?

Oscar knew he had probably assembled this image by borrowing features of current movie stars, famous paintings of women and myth, images from the poetic traditions of courtly love and romance. And certainly girls he'd seen must have contributed--Carol, the sophomore who read *Lady Chatterley's Lover*, Betty translated into a more sensuous being in her own painting, his cousin Elsa glowing as she played the piano.

But tonight, a specific memory was emerging from these sunset clouds and shadows, a face he'd encountered, remembered, and then put away in the back of his mind for inspiration. He knew who this was! The girl he'd met at the bookstore in St. Louis.

On his trip to get a taste of big city life, he, a Midwestern small-town native, had met--briefly, to be sure--a woman who regularly took the train into New York, probably shopped on Fifth Avenue, attended plays on Broadway. Taking the essay by Mark Twain, "The Platonic Sweetheart," from his into her hands, she had connected him for a moment to a scene of important people and stirring events. Her striking looks had retreated to the dark recesses of his memory and been stored as a symbol of future fulfillment.

"Lost in the clouds?" Alice said, smiling down at Oscar. Bob was holding the door open for her. Oscar had not been aware of their approach.

"Oh! You know, daydreaming . . . Good evening. And . . . well, shall we dance?"

"I assume you mean after we get your date, Romeo."

"Right."

Oscar thought red-haired Janet was as inspirational as the sunset. Her long dark dress fell gracefully along her slender body, showing her athletic shape. And she walked with the confidence of a model coming down the runway at Lacy's Department Store. Only he knew that she could vault over a standing saxophone player in a single bound!

The dance was advertised as formal, but the students encouraged Jimmy Glyde and the Gliders (a big band from Kansas City) to play the latest lively tunes so they could jitterbug and do the Lindy Hop. Oscar's group, which performed in between sets, stayed with slower jazz tunes and ballads.

That schedule suited Janet, as she mostly wanted to do the fast numbers. And he was glad he'd been practicing to big band broadcasts in his attic room. He would have liked to hold her close more and maybe sing in her ear, but swing dancing with her turned out to be almost as tantalizing. Her red hair swung out as she spun at the end of his arm, and her dress slid up fine, long legs with regularity.

In a pause between numbers, they were approached by Betty and Henrik. The girls were soon engrossed in a discussion of classes and the professors. Oscar asked about Henrik's family.

"They are well, working all the time, of course. Dad and Uncle Lars think building is

206

finally starting to pick up. Will your father go back to working with them?"

"I know he'd love to leave the mill, even though it's been stable through the worst. But if he gives up a regular job and things don't work out, Mother will never forgive him."

Henrik looked out at the band, which was picking up instruments and about to play. "They're worried about Grandfather, back in Sweden. No one's heard from him or about him for months."

"That's not unusual, though, is it? Aunt Kristina should be able to learn what's happening over there."

"I guess so. It was before our time that he came over here and was so homesick. He might have finally found someone to take care of him after this many years and just doesn't write."

"Well, Father's not said anything about this. I'll ask him."

The band's vocalist stepped up to the microphone, and Oscar could tell from the opening notes she was about sing "Over the Rainbow." He told Henrik, "It's time for us to dance with the girls of our dreams."

As if on cue, Janet whisked him away, and he took advantage of the slow number to let his hand on her waist slip a bit lower than usual and to lean his head close to hers, where he could smell her hair and hum the popular melody.

"You remember our bet?" she asked after a while, tilting her head so that her lips were close to his ear.

"I remember that you claimed we had one."

"And we did. Whoever won the high jump had to . . . "

He was leading, of course, but when he paused to hear what she would say, she steered him into nice little spin.

"Had to . . . ?"

She leaned back and looked into his eyes mischievously. "Had to let the other look up her dress. Now, aren't you sorry you lost?" Despite all the movie scenes he'd written in his head, where the hero's lines escalate to show his cleverness, Oscar could find nothing to say then or later.

"Your date's catching the eye of a lot of boys," Bob told him in another of the pauses. Oscar was on the small stage arranging his music; Prairie Heaven would begin one of its three sessions shortly. "But you're keeping up with her!"

"Thanks. You and Alice make a nice couple." Oscar hesitated at the end of this sentence, mentally trying to construct a better compliment. But then he said, "Well, will you look at that!"

Oscar was staring at the auditorium's entrance, through which the very large Tank and the diminutive Beth Shi were walking. The football star had a characteristic broad smile, and his date more shyly kept her eyes down where she stepped.

He wasn't surprised to see Tank looking this handsome in an elegant suit, but Beth's beauty was remarkable, given the subdued manner and simple dress he associated with her from Miss Young's Studio. Her dancer's figure, a dress that had an Oriental touch, and the reserved manner made her seem a virginal Eastern princess being presented to a European king's son.

It would turn out this couple were even more captivating when they danced. Oscar was especially impressed by their smooth, graceful, movement, always in touch with the dance floor but as if it were some frictionless surface used in a physics experiment. Tank and Beth would also provide the most memorable moment of the dance for many, when she did a graceful backbend, reminding Oscar of Harriet Hoctor in the Gershwin scored movie.

Oscar could not feel jealous, though, with his provocative date also inspiring envious glances from a number of boys. And Janet politely turned down requests to dance when Oscar was playing, reserving herself, as she told him at one point, for the one "who brung her."

Later in the evening, when Prairie Heaven finished "They Can't Take That Away from Me," Oscar smiled out at the crowd again, as the group's members agreed to do. He was pleased to see Tank applauding. When Oscar's gaze reached him, Tank lifted his hands conspicuously in congratulations. What, thought Oscar, a nice--if surprising--gesture.

The night only got better. Prairie Heaven felt optimistic that they had improved their prospects for more contracts. Oscar found Bob's Alice to be a pleasant, intelligent girl who put his friend, often awkward in social situations, completely at ease. He wondered if she were older than her escort.

As the evening came to a close, Oscar was collecting Janet's coat from the cloak room and felt a hand catch him by the arm. It was Tank, who pulled him aside.

"I'm going to need a favor from you," he whispered, glancing around to be sure no one would overhear. "And it's a big one."

Chapter Twenty-nine: Crashes

That night Tank would not discuss the favor he wanted. But Oscar remembered him saying-- after he'd pulled Oscar from the path of an oncoming car--"Now you owe me." This had been preferable to Tank's pulverizing him in revenge for the knockdown at the fair. So he agreed to hear Tank out when it was time.

Their brief exchange moved to the background of Oscar's thoughts the next day, though, when he learned that Professor Lewis was leaving Wesleyan. He later came to see that announcement as the first in a series of revelations that brought down the scenarios of the future he'd been concocting.

"Right now? And where's he going?" Oscar asked Elsa, who'd given him the news at a family gathering in Assyria. Carl had come out to talk with his brothers about the prospects for new work, and Oscar didn't want to be trapped at home all day with his mother. He knew she wanted to talk about him and Betty.

"He says the world is descending into war, a 'veritable death spiral,' he calls it. He's going to volunteer to be a pilot."

"But he's a musician. The artists and the writers lift the rest of us up. They can't become . . . cannon fodder lying in a heap on the battlefield."

They were standing together by a vegetable garden, spaded but not yet planted with spring crops. In the field beyond, winter wheat was rising to sunlight.

"I told him his hands were too precious to go to war, but he said no one can exempt himself from what is coming. And he wants to inspire others to join the cause."

Oscar was irritated. "There is no cause yet. Countries in the Old World are going to eat each other up as they've always done. That's why Aunt Kristina led the way in coming here, where we can be free and build our own lives."

In his head he heard the lyrics to Kate Smith's popular recent rendition of "God Bless America": "While the storm clouds gather far across the sea, / Let us swear allegiance to a land that's free."

His anger was also shaped by the unconscious belief in generational progress he had absorbed from both sides of his family: immigrants who work with their hands come first; their children get education and move up into the professions; and their children institutionalize a higher status and greater fortune. Forces outside our country shouldn't disrupt this process.

"What happens to your music?" Oscar asked his cousin, perhaps to suggest that she would be a victim of her teacher's folly.

"He says I am quite good enough now to be play for our church. And there will be a replacement. We girls, you know, do not become famous. We look up to the boys like you who will make the family proud."

He knew she was right in this, but he still felt Professor Lewis was betraying those who had put their trust in him. Oscar's own rise would not be helped by a pilot who'd be gone from Salinas for years, even if he never got into battle. (Sadly, his friend did not travel far at all. He died in a Colorado training accident in less than a year.)

On the ride home Carl, hearing about Oscar's teacher, was even more subdued than usual. Rather than driving straight home, he stopped at the Salinas air field outside of town. Oscar knew his father sometimes liked to rest here and watch planes land and take off. It was also where Professor Leicht stored his sailplane.

His hands resting on the wheel, Carl asked, "I explained the scar on my leg, ja?"

"Yes, from the motorcycle accident, though you told Mother it came from a childhood incident--falling off a sled." Oscar noticed his father's injured thumb on the wheel.

Carl rubbed his forehead and brought his fingers down across his eyes. "That's not true, but I also didn't get the injury from a motorcycle."

"Oh?" That his father, who never needed to falsify, had told him a lie was unsettling.

"You know that I was in the Swedish Army. We all were."

"Yes, universal conscription."

"Most of that life was routine. We would drill, march, practice, study procedure. And I was able to learn skills. It's how I found I was good with tools and wood."

"The trade that you brought with you to America."

"Ja. Well, one time was different. There had been trouble along the border for some years, with Norway. That country was ruled by our king, and they wanted to be independent. Most of the time the discussions were peaceful, but now and then there would be . . . incidents."

Carl paused as a crop duster came in to land. The pilot's head was visible as the bi-plane glided down to the runway, and Oscar recalled what it was like to be in the second seat of a glider, silently riding the thermal air currents.

"The newspapers didn't tell about these . . . skirmishes. In those days they were fearful that it would lead to more unrest. And sometimes the military--the Army--was called in to restore order. One of those times I had to use my ability."

Oscar couldn't figure out what he meant. Was he to build a fortification, a jail, a catapult? "They needed a special structure?"

"No, they needed a man who could shoot well."

"Ah!" Oscar recalled the demonstration his father had given him in Clay Center.

214

"Two of the agitators had barricaded themselves in the livery of a village near Halden." Oscar had no idea where that was. "They were threatening to set the building on fire, even if it mean they would die in the flames. With the wind that day, many businesses and houses would have burned."

"So, you were supposed to meet their demands?"

"Ja. They wanted one of their fellows released from jail. And the local forces didn't have enough experienced men to take on these agitators who were well armed."

"So, what did you . . . what did the Army do?"

"We shot them. I shot them. I was good with a rifle, you see. And my commander knew that. He had me climb the church tower, and from there I could see them easily. They didn't even know I was up there at first, a sniper."

Carl's intonation seldom varied, but when he delivered the word "sniper" as if it were uttering a curse, with himself the person to be damned.

"Well, you only followed orders. You didn't have a choice."

Again, Carl's hand swept across his face, and his eyes closed. "That is what I know. And I would have been executed myself if I had not obeyed."

215

He paused for such a long time that Oscar had to ask. "But . . . "

"Up there, all alone, as I told you, I could see the two men they wanted me to shoot. I knew them. I had worked with them in the coal mine before I went in to the Army. They were not bad boys, those two. They just wanted their country to be free. They wanted to be free themselves, like I am now and so you are."

Oscar didn't want him to have to say it all. "So, is this also the time when you hurt your leg, got that scar?"

"Hah! Yes, it is. You see, when I shot the first man, he went down right away. But I had to reload, and the second man, he saw where the shot had come from. I don't know if he recognized me, but he looked up and knew what was going to happen. Before I had my gun ready, he signaled an accomplice we hadn't known about. He was in the church below me.

"So, if there was only one way down from the tower, you were in trouble."

"Ja. And what he did was set fire to the wooden stairway leading up to the steeple. The rest of the building was stone, so the fire did not spread . . . when it was all over. But after I fired my second shot, I found I could not go back the way I'd come. I had to climb out onto the slate roof, slide down to the edge, and drop from there. I was lucky not to break any bones on the way to

216

the ground, but I ripped up this leg pretty good on the guttering, I will tell you that."

"After what happened to Uncle John in the Great War, I can see why you never told Mother."

Oscar recalled the many times the two men had been in quiet conversation with each other, Aunt Agnes and his mother working in the kitchen.

"But I carry the memory of what I did in this leg." He rubbed his trousers.

Oscar looked out over the runway where a flock of crows was circling. He knew the conclusion he was supposed to make: he should never put himself in the position his father had been, even if the whole world erupted in war.

Chapter Thirty: Journeys

Several weeks after the dance, Oscar, full of confidence from his last win in table tennis, met Lee at the Y for a rematch. He was also still buoyed by several extended post-dance sessions of kissing and more with Janet, one in the rumble seat of the Peterson's Chevy. But he lost three games in succession by large margins. To make matters worse, Betty and Elsa, there to cheer him on, were far too energetic in offering explanations for the lopsided outcome.

"Lee went back to see his cousins in Wichita," explained Betty, "and playing with them really lifted his game."

Oscar admitted, "He did seem to have adopted a new strategy, taking my shots earlier and keeping his returns so low I couldn't get any power into mine."

Elsa added, "I'm sure your concentration is still being affected by Professor Lewis' decision to join the Army, with everything's that's happening overseas." She chewed her lower lip and looked away, perhaps suggesting that Oscar was weighing his own options for the future.

"We all have a lot to be worried about," agreed Betty. "Lee . . . um, no, it was Beth who told me she has concerns about their family back in China. The Japanese seem to be especially bad to Christians in that country."

Elsa said, "We have family problems, too, Betty. Maybe Henrik has told you, but our Aunt Kristina can't locate our grandfather back in Sweden. She's sent telegrams to the one uncle who's there, but he wrote that Grandfather seems to have disappeared. He said he was going down to the village where he was a child, but they can't find find him."

"Oh," said Oscar, "he'll turn up. They're not very good at record keeping in the Old Country." He rose from the table. "Meanwhile, I'm going to figure out what I need to do to change the record of my matches with Lee! Bye, Elsa. Betty, I guess I'll see you Saturday."

"Yes, the usual time. Mr. Hedd is still preoccupied, and that means more for us to do."

Everyone's preoccupied, thought Oscar, as he left the Y. Father was debating whether to stay on at the mill or take a chance going back to work with his brothers. After hearing again from Agnes in Jefferson City, Mother was distracted by the increasingly likely prospect that her brother would be institutionalized. And Janet wasn't going with him to the movies this weekend because she feared she wasn't doing well enough in her advanced geometry course.

He'd told Bob he'd help with the goats if he'd accompany him to *Only Angels have Wings* with Rita Hayworth and Cary Grant; but his friend, too, had other concerns. Oscar explained how Grant's character is a resigned pilot with whom a female piano player (Jean Arthur) falls in love. "There's all this spectacular flying over and through mountains."

"I can't," Bob had replied. "Alice wants me to go with her when she meets the Higher Life girls at St. Mary's." She had organized the Protestant day-students who took classes there. "I don't want to disappoint her."

"You're not more of a church person than I am. Don't you think you ought to be honest?"

Bob seemed to mull this over. "I've told her . . . in so many words. But, you know what, Oscar? She seems so sure of herself, so mature, maybe it comes from connecting with others who feel the way you do. The girls are drawn to her."

Oscar thought the right man could draw women to him. In the movie, Cary Grant does a favor for another pilot's wife, played by Rita Hayworth; that woman may have feelings for him.

Bob had told Oscar about Higher Life before. This group had discovered a need to get together during the week and took that name because they wanted to rise above a worship of material things, what they thought were the idols of Catholicism.

"You mean you're going to fake it so you can keep taking her to dances . . . and parking at the end of her lane in the moonlight."

Bob slugged him on the shoulder. "You haven't exactly objected to the practice, have you,

'Holier Than Thou.'" Oscar laughed and slugged him back.

Walking home from the Y and lamenting a weekend with no friend or girlfriend to lift his spirits, Oscar met Tank coming out of the Red Dragon.

"Ah, just the man I want to see," said the big man, clapping him on the shoulder.

"Oh? You've been to another meal in there?" Oscar gestured toward the restaurant.

"Yes . . . and no. I was meeting a friend. Actually, I might as well tell you. Let me walk along with you."

"Sure. I'm just headed home."

"Tell you the truth, Squarehead, I've been seeing Beth Shi, your friend Lee's sister, quite a bit. Well, for some time, too."

Oscar was surprised, believing Tank came back from school only occasionally. And, to his mind, dating Beth would be stepping down a social level or two from the beauties he could have as a star athlete."Ah. I know her, too. We both work at the High Pointe."

"Um-hm. Are you aware of the family history?"

"Not really. They came from Wichita is about all I understand."

"They do have family there, but they really come from Nanking, in China. Have you heard about what the Japanese are doing?"

"They're taking over parts of the country, right?"

"Yes. It's been a brutal campaign, especially in Nanking." Tank actually shuddered when he said this. "They slaughtered thousands, hundreds of thousands--men, women, and children. Drove some of them into pits and just shot them or set fire to them or buried them alive."

"Can that be true? I haven't read anything about it or heard it on the radio." Oscar knew, though, that he didn't pay that much attention to international news.

"People here don't believe the stories, and it's even worse than killing. What they did to the women . . . well, I can't repeat it. But I've heard it all from the Shi family. They were among the few lucky ones who escaped. A small band of European and American people set up a safety zone in the city, and the Shis--well, most of the family--were taken in."

"I thought they'd been in this country a lot longer than that. Lee and Beth speak such good English and seem to know a lot about America."

"They learned from missionaries, especially one American woman." He stopped and stared off in space a moment. "Did you know, by the way, that their restaurant is modeled on the Gate of Maternal Virtues, erected by an emperor long ago in honor of his mother? There's a poem about her spirit painted into the design. Women can be heroes sometimes."

Oscar wouldn't have used that term, but now that he thought about it, Aunt Agnes might be heroic. "I've felt that there was a sadness about Beth, a sorrow she could not name."

They walked on in silence for half a block. Then Tank stopped and turned to Oscar. "I tell you all this so I can ask you that favor I told you about."

"Okay."

"I need you to give me some of your urine."

"What?"

"I'm enlisting in a special military unit that's going to send me . . . well, to some places I can't tell you about. It's top secret. And only after months of training, maybe years. But I have a problem with the physical. Sometimes I have blood in my urine. I'm pretty sure it's because of football, how hard I work and the contact. There's nothing really wrong with me, but I'm afraid if I go in--and I need to go this month--they'll find blood, and I'll be rejected."

"So I'm to disguise myself as you and fill up a vial? I don't think that will work."

"No, it's simple. You piss in a little bottle an hour before I report. I have a way of keeping it hidden on my body. When the time comes, I'll transfer your urine into the specimen bottle."

Oscar had long seen himself as a man who did not have to follow the rules designed for ordinary men, so he wasn't held back by a strict social code. It was odd, though, that, in a sense, he--or his urine--would be enlisting in the military, to do what acts he couldn't even know.

"You're sure no one will find out?"

"I'm sure. And if someone was suspicious, I swear to you I would never mention your name. You're a good guy, after all, Oscar. And . . . I'll be grateful for as long as I live."

As long as he lives? Oscar hoped Tank wasn't thinking this was a short term project. But, after giving it some thought, he agreed to this completely unexpected request. The bigger surprise for him came when he got home. His mother met him at the door, pulled him to her, and said, "You and I must be strong, Oscar. Your father is going back to Sweden, and we're moving to Missouri."

"How could it be," thought Oscar, "that everywhere I walk in Jefferson City is uphill?"

He was trudging from his grandparents' home to his aunt's cafe on McCartney Street, and the last three blocks were a climb, seeming steeper because of the heat. But he was ignoring a rule of physics he understood well in theory: if he left a point at a certain elevation and traveled to another at the same elevation, each step up was matched by a step down.

Also aware of the geographic data, he would have to admit that coming from Salinas, at 1224 feet above sea level, to Jefferson City (638 feet) had been a downhill journey, like that of Rocky Mountain water descending in the Kansas and Missouri Rivers. Oscar's walking and bike riding over the previous few years had involved few ups and downs, as Salinas was flat.

Of course, what truly irritated him this summer in his wanderings was that he was not in Salinas, not at Wesleyan, not pursuing his dream of greatness. He was with his mother and grandparents, awaiting his father's return from the Old Country.

The door to the Ridgetop Cafe was propped open in the summer heat, and the kitchen stoves raised the temperature more as the cook prepared the evening's main dishes. Oscar walked in and took a stool. "Coffee?" his aunt Agnes asked.

"Yes. And make it strong."

"Ah, bad day so far or long night ahead?"

He'd gotten a temporary job at the River Bottom Theater, which was not located by the Missouri River but near the little creek that fed Sunset Lake. His taking tickets, keeping an eye on patrons, and cleaning up didn't pay much, but he saw movies for nothing and every penny he earned helped him and his mother.

The rest of the Lindbloom family had contributed toward a fund that was financing Carl's travels to the home country and supporting Sallie while he was gone. But her anger at the entire situation had led to her decision to spend this time with Oscar's grandparents. Her son worked to help meet expenses but also in order to be out of the house as much as was reasonable.

"Both bad day and long night," he told his aunt, who had become a chief confidant in his new situation. "I've had the matinee, and we're playing at Eddie's Basement." He had joined two cousins and one of their friends in a little combo that entertained bar customers from early evening until late at night. Their music was conventional, but occasionally Oscar got to break away in a blues solo, expressing his unhappiness in unusual rhythms and minor keys.

"You need to meet a girl," Aunt Agnes said. "Someone to listen to you play and take you to church the next day."

"It's hard to meet a proper girl where we perform. But if you know of one, please tell me where I might find her." He would not want one who would take him to church, of course. And Aunt Agnes was not truly worried about him but was probably indirectly expressing a desire that his wayward cousins be rescued by an angel of mercy.

Oscar actually had a girl, or at least he had his eye on a girl. Touring the state capitol building on one of his first days in town, he'd stood on the ground floor looking up at paintings on the rotunda ceiling. Beside an older gentleman on a high balcony was a young woman in a dark business suit. Oscar could see her shapely legs up to the knee.

He saw her twice more--once on a second visit to the capitol, where she was the only woman in a circle of men, most probably legislators. The last occasion was at Eddie's.

"It's possible," he thought the first time he noticed her, "that this man is the very governor of Missouri, and she is one of his closest aides deciding who will receive prestigious awards at an upcoming ceremony."

The woman, a dark-haired beauty with an intriguing Mediterranean look, was holding a clipboard and a pen. The gentleman spoke quietly

227

to her, looking ahead as he walked. There was an easiness in the pair's conversation, as if she shared in the power he wielded. Oscar wanted to be that man of authority and be adored by such a woman.

He had expected to be charming Janet Middleton this summer as he prepared for his last year at college, a year that would gain him honors and catapult him to advanced study at a major university. Before leaving town, he had urged Bob to let him know what she was doing while he was gone so he could tailor his letters to her, following up on the dates they had had. He hoped not to be gone long.

It had taken Carl two weeks to journey from Kansas to Gotenburg. There he'd sent a post card that he was on his way to the village where his father was last reported to have been. He hoped to track Lars down, make sure he was provided for, and return home in three to four weeks. Until he was back, Sallie and Oscar would stay in Jefferson City.

"Aunt Agnes," he asked, "are your customers mostly state workers? Or are the people I see here from businesses downtown?"

"Some of both. The shop owners and bigwigs, they eat at the Skyview." That was the elegant hotel only a block away, famous for its escalators. "But we have our regulars."

He was thinking about how well she managed her business. "Um-hum. Did you plan to go to college before Uncle John joined the Army?"

"Yes, I did. You know that my father was a successful banker, and we had enough money, even after my brothers finished their schooling. I didn't enroll, though, because your uncle told me he'd wind up 'that war' in no time and be back home to take care of me."

She was still taking care of him in the little house next door, but the decision had finally been made to move John to the Old Soldiers' Home in the fall. He probably wouldn't know the difference any more, she said.

"Would you have studied business?"

She laughed. "No, I wanted to be an artist."

"A painter?" He recalled the fine pictures Betty had done.

"I wanted to be be a potter, to create perfect forms out of clay."

Oscar had seen potters at work, their hands covered in mud and their aprons smeared. Painters kept such mess at brush's length. Music and poetry were even better media, putting pure sounds and fine words together. Scraping up congealed spills under theater seats and wading through beery sawdust on the bar floor had fired Oscar's zeal to work in pure forms.

When he looked at the Thomas Hart Benton mural along the walls of the capitol building,

Oscar identified with the well-dressed men leaning on canes, smoking cigars, reading books. In an odd way, though, he could admire Frankie shooting Johnny, Jessie James holding up a train, and Jim escaping with Huck. Unlike the men working in the fields, on the railroad, and along the riverfront, they were seizing their own destiny rather than working for others.

Oscar remained confident that he was in control of his own fate, especially after flooring a rowdy customer in a barroom brawl. As at the county fair some years earlier, the brief encounter with Tank made him believe he could always take decisive control of a situation if necessary. While his earlier boxing strategy had been inspired by his adolescent fascination with Edgar Rice Burroughs' heroes, this one had a real life model-- Henry Armstrong.

Stories about Armstrong, who had grown up in St. Louis, were all over Missouri papers. Part Indian, part Negro, he was both welterweight and light heavyweight champion of the world; and, at one point, he had knocked out twenty-seven opponents in a row. Oscar liked the neatness of a knockout, but he had also learned, sparring with boxers at Wesleyan, that body punches win more fights than blows to the head.

So, when a drunken customer at Eddie's Basement went out of control, Oscar brought him down with punishing blows to the midsection. He would also claim that he, older and wiser after a broken wrist, was avoiding damage to his musician's fingers.

Eddie's bouncer, a reformed Irish alcoholic, had been escorting another contentious drinker to the street when Oscar took a restroom break. In the hallway he came upon a man pressing his forearm into the back of a woman, her face mashed into the wall. The attacker's other hand had disappeared up the back of her dress.

Oscar stepped up beside him, and delivered two left hooks to his side. When the man turned to face him, Oscar threw three successive punches to his middle, and the man crumbled to the floor. Oscar had sized him up quickly and correctly-- overweight, middle-aged, intoxicated.

"Sorry about that," Oscar said to the woman, whom he'd not recognized at first. She had spun around, pushing her dress down. Less distressed than he expected, she gave him a crooked smile and said simply, "Thanks."

That's when he realized this was the same woman he had seen on the balcony and on the floor of the state capitol.

"I'm Mattie," she said without giving a last name.

"Oscar," he replied, wanting to, but not adding, "What's a lady like you doing in a place like this?" Instead, he said, "You okay?"

"Yes. I don't know what brought that on. But he'd been leering at me most of the night."

"You're by yourself?"

Oscar saw Small Harry, the bouncer (who was not small), looking down the hall at the man on the floor, still unable to get up. Seeing Mattie fixing her hair in a pocket mirror and Oscar's protective pose, he escorted Mattie's assailant up the entrance stairs and away with such conviction that it was unlikely he would come back that night . . . or perhaps ever..

Mattie explained, "I came with a friend, but he . . . had to leave. I had just finished my drink and stepped back here to . . . ."

"I see. Hey, I have to play this set out, but, if you need a walk . . . to where you're going, I won't be more than about forty-five minutes."

"You're very kind. I'm at the Towers, just a few blocks, but . . . " She chewed her lower lip. " . . . if you wouldn't mind?" He smiled his assent and rejoined the band.

The Towers was where many successful young government workers and office holders resided. It was expensive, but, now that Oscar thought about it, Mattie's clothes matched that style. Neither her outfit nor her manner belonged with the clientele of Eddie's Basement, and he tried to think back and visualize who her escort might have been.

He also looked ahead to figure out how he could get away from Sam and Carney, his cousins. They liked to take money from the tip jar and extend their fun in even less reputable establishments than Eddie's. They had already said he should go with them tonight.

For all his mother's pride in her family, there were individuals past and present she preferred not to acknowledge. Sam and Carney were sons of her brother Edgar, a Baptist minister; and conventional lore about preachers' children needing to rebel seemed to apply in their case.

For several years the twins had been slipping away from their home on the northeastern edge of the city, following the railroad tracks into town, and carousing. Had they not been her brother's sons, Sallie would have called them "low life." As it was, she avoiding speaking directly about them.

"Your father's away now," she told Oscar when he explained that he was going to play the saxophone for Undertones. "I want you to be careful who you're with and where you go. You can trust your Uncle Edgar, of course, . . . but not everyone in his family."

The Reverend Edgar Bahr not only held together the small flock of The Church of the Risen Lord but also served as a part-time chaplain at the Missouri State Penitentiary, the place where some insisted his boys would eventually reside.

"I'll come straight home after we close," Oscar had assured her. And he'd been careful to make his getaways prompt both times he'd played with them. The truth was he had no desire to visit the dives Sam and Carney told him about during their breaks.

However, the stories they told did arouse his curiosity about the darker elements of society, especially when they involved (or so it was claimed) beautiful women drawn to forceful and daring men. The brunette Oscar had seen walking the halls of power--who had showed up in Eddie's Basement--might represent an intriguing intersection of propriety and recklessness, not unlike the subjects of lurid dramas concocted by the Bahr brothers.

Oscar had to assume that the man he'd seen with Mattie on the balcony of the state capital was, if not the governor, surely an important figure. He would have aides, male and female, whose hands got dirty doing his work. How low, he wondered, had she gone--or been dragged--to gain power?

234

For a moment, Oscar considered courting such power himself, maybe just long enough to guarantee his own autonomy. With his genius, it couldn't take too many years to rise to the top, retire with an admiring wife in the dream home Musica Universalis, and pursue his own interests without restraint.

When he saw *Mr. Smith Goes to Washington*, he concluded that the hero's idealism was inspiring, but that in the end he is saved more by the efforts of other people than by his own decency. And it's not clear if his struggle led to a better world, either for the boys he wanted to help or for himself. Should he enter public life one day, Oscar believed he would be more shrewd in sizing up politicians, more resourceful in maneuvering his course, more decisive in action.

"Come with us to the Sink Hole," Sam said as Oscar was swabbing his horn. "There's a girl there we want you to meet." He winked at Carney.

"It's more she wants to meet you, 'Scar. We told her you was handsome, a college boy."

"That's mighty nice of you, but I promised to walk the lady home." Oscar nodded toward Mattie, standing by the door.

"Oh, that's fine. You get Miss Angel where she needs to be, and we'll be waitin'. The night's young, 'Scar, and you can tell Aunt Sallie you were watching out for us. You know, keeping us on the up and up."

The brothers had nicknamed him 'Scar when he foolishly told them about Tarzan's injury in the fight with Terkoz. It reddened when the Ape Man got mad and was a sign to anyone who knew him to get out of his way.

"Tell you what, then, once I'm sure she's safe and home, I'll try to drop by."

They knew he wouldn't, but they'd been taken aback a bit by the ability of their cousin as he expertly dispatched the unruly customer. They were sure they could have handled the situation, too, but Oscar had risen in their estimation and they decided he might not be as easy to lead down their path to mischief as they had thought.

"I like your music," Mattie offered as they stepped out of Eddie's. "You must have started young to play so well . . . at your age."

"Well, I play for fun, really. I'll be going to graduate school in another year, not to study music but probably science."

"You'll go if the country doesn't go to war."

He wasn't happy to have the conversation heading in this direction so quickly, but then again, if she worked at the capitol, questions about preparations and contingencies were probably on her mind routinely. "That's all over there. Let them have their conflicts."

Now that they had left the neighborhood of Eddie's, he was happy to see there were other well-dressed people on the sidewalks. "You're at the Towers; do you work downtown?"

"Yes. I'm in the government. The governor's office, in fact."

"Ah, a right-hand man."

She laughed. "No, I'm definitely lower echelon. I even make the coffee."

From where they were on High Street, Oscar could see the outline of the state penitentiary building against the night sky. "The Walls" was an imposing structure, looming over the Missouri River and the Missouri Pacific railroad tracks along its banks. His cousins loved to regale each other--and anyone within earshot--with tales of mayhem inside the prison. They bragged that their father passed on the shocking tales of what went on behind bars.

Public hangings had just been outlawed in Missouri and a gas chamber erected inside the facility; so the final minutes of condemned men-- and women--were witnessed by only a few, such as a chaplain. The brothers' accounts of executions by the new method varied from chilling to idealized fantasy, from horrible writhing and cursing to prayer becoming peaceful slumber.

After Oscar saw *Each Dawn I Die* with James Cagney, he imagined the interior of that huge penitentiary through scenes from the movie. He pictured the hero, having been beaten by guards, spending months in "The Hole," handcuffed to bars and given only bread and water. He created even more graphic mental images of Cagney's plight using Sam and Carney's description of the death row cells, deep below ground level in the pen.

"The Court's not too many blocks from my aunt's restaurant, the Ridgetop Cafe. Ever been there?"

"I think I've walked by--on McCartney?"

"Yes, It's small, but the food's decent and price . . . well, a student can afford to eat there."

"Ah, a family place. I'd like to try it." She sighed deeply. "Sometimes, where I work, it can be so cutthroat, I forget what it's like to be with people you trust."

A summer romance? Oscar had been so focused on what he was missing back in Salinas that it hadn't occurred to him his weeks in a different town might provide the opportunity for a brief but intense love affair.

And here was an undoubtedly attractive woman, doing well in life but perhaps feeling cut off from the simplicity and decency of her childhood. Oscar resented looking young to her (even though he was not as old as most men beginning their last year of college), but if she was eager to find the clean-cut, All-American type . . . why, he could play that role.

Not, of course, that she would jump into his arms without some clever wooing on his part. But he decided he could at least determine if the governor's assistant (or whatever her title was) would be interested in getting to know a young man with many talents.

Though he saw no ring on her left hand, for all he knew she could have a steady beau. Someone had been her escort at Eddie's. But if that man had not felt obligated to stay, the two could simply have been associates meeting to talk politics or business.

He thought about Johnny Case (Cary Grant) in the movie, *Holiday*, who weighs the merits of marrying a woman (Doris Nolan) with money and connections or her sister (Katharine Hepburn), who finds pleasure in everyday experiences. Janet Middleton enjoyed high-jumping, dancing, and teasing; a beautiful woman in Jefferson City worked with people who determined how the resources of the state were allocated. Would he get to choose between the two?

Oscar came to the front entrance of The Towers, on the top of a wide semi-circular, railed porch. She turned and offered him her hand. "It's Mattie Hill, by the way. You've been kind."

"Oscar Lindbloom. I just did . . . what had to be done. Glad I was there."

Her smile told him to smile back and leave, which he did. Still, he thought this exchange encouraging. He couldn't see himself marching back to her residence--or the capitol, for that matter--and asking to see Miss Hill without a reasonable pretext, but he would try to come up with one.

As Oscar approached his grandparents' house off Swift's Highway (a steep, uphill path he was too preoccupied to complain about this time), there at least appeared to be more promising prospects for the weeks and months ahead than he'd thought. In the meantime, however, he knew he had to keep his mother content.

"I heard you come in last night," Sallie told him the next morning. Oscar slept on what had been a back porch, recently closed in for a storage room. His grandparents had put a cot in the little room off the kitchen because his mother needed the second bedroom. He liked it that, if he were careful, he could enter and exit through the back door without everyone knowing.

"I came straight home. We have to put away our music and instruments, you know. And then there's the walk back."

"We didn't get any mail yesterday. I do so worry about Carl! Do you think he's found his father? He could have had an accident."

"Mother, he's fine. No one can take care of himself better than Father, you know that. But we have to give him time."

Because they'd thought six weeks would be the outside range of his absence, Mr. Hedd said he, with Betty's help, would hold Oscar's job for him. And school would not resume until September, so he had concluded that, when Carl returned--surely before the end of summer--all would be well.

"The country over there is rough. He's told me--mountains and raging rivers crashing down to the sea. His father, Lars, may be in some remote little village in a forgotten valley somewhere, and Carl could fall down a cliff trying to get there."

"Mother, we shouldn't be thinking like that. Isn't today when you're going to Uncle Sam's? That will be a nice time."

Both Uncle Edgar and Uncle Sam lived on the eastern part of town, where houses were farther apart and the landscape resembled the country they had grown up in down near Iberia.

"Yes, but I do wish you'd come with me. Your cousins, Ida and Minnie, will be there. They're younger than you, but such sweet girls."

Because of Oscar's success at school and his father's being away, Sallie was more timid than she'd been in the past. She gave fewer commands and made more requests.

"I promised Aunt Agnes I'd draw up her new menu for her. It's a nice sketch of the Governor's mansion that can be traced on each one. I'll go with you next time."

Oscar had accompanied his mother to the obligatory family events in the first week after they arrived. Then the two jobs gave him excuses to be elsewhere; and sometimes he fabricated "practice sessions" for Undertones and "learning new procedures" at the River Bottom.

He also didn't like the part of town his uncles lived in, a low area south of the bluffs along the Missouri River. A creek wound down one edge of their joint property, and the humidity was a sharp contrast with hot and mostly dry Kansas. So long as Sallie was occupied with reminiscing about family history and waiting for the mail, he felt justified in being away from home, a young man out on the town.

The hardest visit was with Aunt Agnes and Uncle John. She, of course, was cheerful and eager to learn more about his hopes and dreams, but Oscar was troubled by the figure of her husband settled into an easy chair in one corner.

When his mother stepped into the kitchen to help prepare sandwiches, he was left alone with his uncle. Even though the Venetian blinds were half closed, John wore dark glasses, so Oscar couldn't tell if he was awake or asleep, listening or dreaming.

"It's warm here," Oscar offered. "In Salinas, we usually have a breeze."

Was the answer a confirmation--"Um-hm"--or a respiratory rattle--"Ohh-ohh"--or some type of snore--"agh-agh"? There was no movement in any part of his body, most of which was covered in an afghan.

Oscar thought of the Smallweeds in Dickens' novel, *Bleak House*. An elderly couple, they were both so infirm that their lives were mostly spent sitting in matching chairs in front of the fire. She was senile, he a nasty old miser. Whenever, in her mindless rambling, Mrs. Smallweed used any term related to money, her husband would throw a pillow at her and knock her back into her chair, senseless.

But the exertion this effort takes causes Mr. Smallweed to sink lower into his own seat, so that the two seem to be vanishing downwards into caves of blankets and cushion. At his command,

243

"Shake me up, Judy!," they are rescued by a resentful granddaughter, whose hoisting is unnecessarily rough. (It's her one act of rebellion to her servitude.)

Oscar looked toward the swinging doors of the kitchen, hoping for rescue. But he suspected the two women might be commiserating about the burdens with which their husbands had left them. One had to become a permanent nursemaid, the other a kind of temporary widow.

"So, I guess you've heard my father has gone back to Sweden to locate his father. The family over here hasn't heard from him in some time. You remember Carl, don't you?"

Again, the answer--if it was an answer--was undistinguishable. Oscar knew his uncle had been in the trenches in Europe, alternately bombarded by artillery shells and facing machine gun fire between the lines. He'd read historical accounts of failed charges across No Man's Land and seen pictures of battlefields strewn with corpses.

"Carl, my father, he was in the Army, too, you know. He's . . . he's told me some of things he had to do. I guess you know about them, too."

This time he felt the sound made by his uncle was clearer. "Yes. Yes."

Again, Oscar checked the door to the kitchen. He heard the clinking of classes and muted conversation.

"He wasn't exactly in a war, but he did have to . . . to use his rifle. Did he ever tell you about that?"

"Yes. Yes."

"It's funny, but he was up in a church steeple, a place of worship. Yet he was firing down at . . . at an enemy. Well, the man wasn't an enemy exactly."

This time Oscar wasn't sure he heard correctly. The "yes, yes" could have been "gas, gas." Or it could have been a cough that meant nothing, a sound no more meaningful than Mrs. Smallweed's "half-pence" or "interest" or "purchases."

"Is everyone ready for lunch?" Aunt Agnes said pleasantly. She held up a tray with both hands, her hip blocking open the door. Oscar's mother followed her with a pitcher of lemonade.

Oscar was ready.

Chapter Thirty-four: Stairways

Before he took the new menu to his aunt, Oscar received surprising news in a letter from Bob back in Salinas.

"Betty Devine sails at the end of the month to be a missionary in China. Her parents tried to talk her out of it, but their minister came to her defense. Beth Shi had connected her with a church in Wichita that has a mission, and that minister assured everyone it would be safe. What I see in the papers doesn't make it sound safe to me!"

Oscar had read *The Good Earth* and thought of China as a backward land where even good people had to cheat and steal to survive. If some families struggled to the top for a brief time, they would be brought low by the next generation, even by their own children. He couldn't imagine Betty volunteering to enter such a world.

He remembered the theater poster for the movie with Luise Rainer and Paul Muni; it showed O-Lan lying on the ground, one hand holding up a blooming branch. It bothered him that the limb was upside down; the stem, broken at its base, was reaching toward the sky while the flowers drooped toward the ground. The heroine, though beautiful, was flat on her back, a symbol to Oscar of being held down by an ancient and backward way of life.

He'd also read Buck's book about her father, *Fighting Angel: Portrait of a Soul*, which showed Westerners to be imperialists. In her view, missionaries, though fiercely dedicated, took advantage of simpler minds. So, even the people who were convincing Betty to bring religion to a faraway place might take advantage of her good will.

His suspicion of churches had been reinforced by the Sacred Heart of Jesus statue, which he passed almost daily on his way to and from the Ridgetop. A sculpted Christ literally pulls open his chest to show his heart. Standing at the foot of the statue, Oscar felt this religion called for believers to sacrifice themselves for an unverifiable reward. Would Betty be hurt far from her family and friends? And what, he wondered, had made her want to make this rash decision?

"Janet is staying close to home," Bob continued. "Alice and I talked to her at the city pool, where she's working as a lifeguard (she looks swell up on her stand in a bathing suit--girl on a pedestal!) She's helping Dr. Bohns in some research program over the summer. She asked about you as if she'd not gotten any letters--you keeping your place in line, Oscar?"

Oscar, who had written faithfully, resented Janet's not acknowledging his almost daily reports. Of course, he sent her poems, dreamy landscape sketches, philosophical discourses on the meaning of existence rather than accounts of what he saw in a new city or what he was doing

247

with his mother's family. It hadn't occurred to him until now that maybe he should have been sending more conventional observations.

The rest of Bob's news concerned the tedium of his own summer job (at his father's company), the fact he was taking Alice on (inexpensive) outings, and an admission that things were a little dull without his best friend in town. Oscar sensed Alice was filling in for him quite well as a source of excitement in Bob's life; so he returned to consideration of his own need for adventure.

Except for the odd appearance of Mattie Hill at Eddie's Basement, that seedy establishment had not made him feel he was encountering anything that hadn't been available in Salinas. And the River Bottom Theater's most memorable moment was discovering an elderly man in the balcony with his hand on a woman's knee--and more. When Oscar requested he behave properly, the man explained with a wink, "She's my wife, Sonny. And she thinks this is proper."

On his way to the Ridgetop, Oscar stopped by the Skyview Hotel to marvel again at their escalator system. Unlike others he'd seen, this one made the works visible by putting a glass wall on the side of the structure. Visitors could watch the machine at work.

Two things struck Oscar about escalator construction: the first was that the steps actually travel on wheels. The top of the step is flat, of course; but the whole is a triangular solid with the bottom edge serving as an axle with two small wheels, one at each end. The wheels ride on guiding rails from bottom to top (or top to bottom).

Another pair of wheels, higher up on the step's side, are connected to the drive chain loop, which, powered by the electric motor, pulls all the steps. The tapering shape of each step allows them to fold together at the top, where they fit into a continuous surface as they circle around the pulling gears, much like a tire on a wheel.

The second feature he liked was the simple fact that there are not really two escalators, an up and a down. Each escalator has both features, but you generally don't see the second function because it's behind a wall, the truss. The chain goes one way for up and is reversed for down. The Skyview's glass wall allowed Oscar to observe the endless cycle of rise and fall the steps took while passengers make their journeys to a floor above or a floor below.

In his design of the dream house--to which he would one day retire with the most beautiful woman in the world--he had pictured circular escalators taking residents from floor to floor in a glass housing. One side of the truss would face an outer wall, also glass, which would give riders a view of the countryside. In the other direction they could see the rooms they were passing through.

At the Ridgetop he found his aunt turning chairs upside down onto table tops, preparing to close the cafe. With two waiters and a cook, she served breakfast and lunch. Agnes helped out with all facets of the operation, but particularly managed the cash register.

Oscar had learned that Uncle John would sleep much of the day, though Agnes stepped next door from time to time to check on him. He was restless from mid-afternoon until night, so she generally began closing at 3:00, stayed an hour or more to prepare for the next day, and then went to the house. As far as Oscar knew, for twenty years, about her only other activity was church on Sunday morning.

She sat down at a table by one wall, and he slid the menu sketch across to her. "What do you think? I made it a little different from others I've seen around town."

His picture was of the interior of the governors' mansion and featured the Grand Stairway carved of walnut. He showed it from base looking upward, the lines elongated and diminishing toward the top. The sketch was uncluttered with detail, almost an architect's blueprint.

"It's very nice." She held it up and looked out at the street. The mansion was only a few blocks away, but the building itself was not visible from where they were. "For years I had a drawing of my building, but, now that I think about it, anyone who is here can see the Ridgetop. This places us in the capitol context."

"That's what I thought. And everyone wants to be climbing up in life, so it's inspiring--at least to me."

Agnes laid the menu on the countertop. "It's the men who look up, Oscar. Young women come down the staircase to meet their callers. Have you met any ladies here who hope you'll be stepping up to the porch and knocking on their door?"

"Now, Aunt Agnes, I've told you I 'left a girl behind' in Salinas." He took the menu back from her and studied it again. "Of course, should some local Katharine Hepburn come walking down this staircase . . . " He pointed. " . . . or in that door, " he gestured over his shoulder, " . . . I'd be quick to pay her the appropriate attention."

He watched his aunt's eyes swing up to the entrance and linger. Was Mattie Hill right now reaching for the handle and about to step inside? There was no reason for Oscar to think so, but no reason not to hope.

She could, he romanticized, be trying to extricate herself from a web of competing forces, different figures in political machines that wanted her assistance in, say, funding a monument to their revered ancestor; building a new skyscraper in Kansas City; or constructing a bridge over the Missouri River. She would be rewarded for her cooperation; but whatever she did would anger those she couldn't please and make her feel she'd dirtied her hands for those she had.

Torn between choices that would destroy her belief in mankind's basic goodness, she would seek protection from an independent man. That man would be a genius, able to lift both of them out of the swampy quagmire of ordinary life.

She would realize that this musician/artist/ philosopher could change the world with his poetry more rapidly and surely than all the legislation passed by state assemblies. He would be the fulfillment of her personal and professional desires.

When he heard a rattle at the door behind him, Oscar couldn't help himself. He turned immediately and saw an older woman waving a handkerchief at him.

Mrs. Britton, who lived on the other side of the Ridgetop, was waving at Agnes, not Oscar. A package from the office of Veterans' Affairs had been delivered to her address by mistake, and she worried that it might be important. It turned out to be more paperwork about John's admittance to the Old Soldiers' Home.

Oscar left his aunt puzzling over the new forms, but he carried with him her commission to trace out a dozen sketches on white cardboard. The dishes and prices would go on the other side. In his heart he also carried the conviction that, as Mattie Hill had not been knocking on the cafe door, he would have to take himself to the Towers.

He was ambushed on his way out of the River Bottom by his fun-loving cousins. "We're on our way to see the Celestial Fanny. Jump in." Sam was driving the family DeSoto, the window down. Both boys had cigarettes hanging down from the corners of their mouths.

"The what?"

"Celeste. She's a stripper. A good one, too. Got tattoos."

Oscar heard Groucho Marx singing *"Lydia, the Tattooed lady"*: "When her muscles start relaxin' / Up the hill comes Andrew Jackson." In

Salinas he would have avoided such an excursion, not wanting to be seen coming, going, or there. But in Jefferson City, who would know? And if Sam or Carney told tales about what they'd done, he, a more skilled storyteller, would cast himself in the role of parole officer to two delinquents.

As they drove through town on Highway 50 going west, the three talked about Undertones and new songs they wanted to learn. While the Bahr twins might raise eyebrows with their antics, there was no question of their musical ability. And Oscar knew their parents hoped talent would lead them eventually to productive roles.

At one point, Carney said, "Hey, 'Scar, you sure did in that guy at the bar the other night! Where did you learn to box? You looked like a professional."

"There's a ring at the Y back in Salinas. And I sparred some at college. But a lot of it you just pick up on your own."

"And did all your opponents crash to the canvas like the groper at Eddie's?"

Oscar laughed, as if he were in fact "'Scar." "Of course. My fists are registered as deadly weapons, you know."

"Hah! Our heads are registered, too. We butt them into walls whenever we get a chance."

They drove some more, turning down increasingly small country roads. "Say, where exactly is this show?" Oscar asked. "I thought it was in town."

"Nah. Little place, The Sink Hole. Just a couple more miles."

Oscar knew about sink holes, places where the land has collapsed after years of underground erosion by water. It can happen suddenly, swallowing buildings and individuals who had thought they were standing on solid ground.

Sometimes, too, sink holes become shut-ins, formations where water flows into rocks and out of sight to join a vast system of underground currents, eventually emerging as a spring or part of an existing river. Missouri has a lot of sink holes, especially where the Missouri joins the Mississippi River north of St. Louis.

Sam drove more than "a few miles" down a winding dirt road through rocky hills into a deep valley. Finally they came to a building with weathered siding, a flat roof--long, and low. On a hand-lettered sign by the Sink Hole door, Oscar read, "Dancing tonight. The Celestial Fanny." He thought to himself that it was unlikely he would see Gypsy Rose Lee. Or Lydia, the Tattooed Lady: " For a dime you can see Kankakee or Paree / Or Washington crossing the Delaware."

Whatever was here, though, the parking lot was so full of cars, they had to turn around and park on the edge of the road, back about fifty yards. The ground was soft, and Oscar hoped they wouldn't be stuck . . . or sink into a gigantic cavern.

On the way in, Sam punched Oscar on the shoulder. "It's gonna' be great, 'Scar, but the crowd now . . . they can get a bit wild."

"I'll remember where the exit is."

His cousins were not about to sit back by the exit if they could help it. They pushed their way along one wall up toward the stage, a plywood platform perhaps three feet high. Oscar felt that the floor slanted down on their side. He decided if he heard any underground rumblings, he would bolt out of the Sink Hole and leave his cousins to fall or climb, every man for himself.

On stage a vaudeville comedian was trying to tell jokes to a restless crowd, mostly men, but here and there a middle-aged woman could be seen with an arm through her escort's.

"So every time this guy hears the word 'sucker,' he goes berserk. But he's selling leeches, see, so when he's closing the deal, his customer always refers to the 'sucker,' and he flies into a rage and loses the sale."

"Give us three beers," said Carney to an overweight waiter who nonetheless moved swiftly. "And a bowl of nuts."

Sam added, "And when's Celeste taking it off?" But the waiter had already disappeared among other tables.

Oscar scanned the crowd, irrationally wondering if Mattie Hill could be there. The cigarette smoke was so thick and the lights so low, he couldn't see the length of the room. And he felt he was looking up through the haze from a depression.

"So, he finally makes a sale to a lady customer, who claims to be deaf. He feels sorry for her and gives her a discount. When she walks away, he bites the coin she gave him and realizes it's a fake. 'Sucker!' she calls out and runs."

The boos had gotten louder, and some men in the back were clapping their hands, calling for the stripper. The bartender signaled the comedian, who was happy to escape; and the band broke into a traditional bump and grind rhythm.

After a delay--one of many teases to come--a tall blonde put a long leg through the curtains; and then the rest of her, in tight riding pants and a jockey's helmet, came out on stage. The second arm to emerge through the curtains held a riding crop. Oscar asked, "Why is she called the 'Celestial Fanny'?"

"Oh, you'll see," said Carney and raised his hand for more beers.

Oscar had read how Gypsy Rose Lee entertained her fans by taking off her clothes and making sharp quips about philosophy, literature, and the arts. She was high-brow and low-brow at the same time, rolling garters down her thigh while reciting lofty passages of poetry.

The Sink Hole sax player began wailing a song Oscar didn't know, but in a Charlie Parker style; and he hummed along with the melody. Celeste, now undulating at the front of the stage, crooned, "Take me out to the racetrack, / I'll ride all your stallions bareback." She pointed a finger at an excited customer and peeled off one glove.

"Oh, I'm the horse for you, Baby," called Sam. "And you won't need no saddle."

Oscar thought Celeste looked Scandinavian. He pictured his cousin Elsa, who loved to ride ponies in Assyria, and laughed to think of her playing the piano for this performance. Celeste threw her second glove behind her, and the band played "Call to the Post."

A waiter brought out an oversized sawhorse with a small racing saddle attached to the top bar, and Celeste swung one leg over and into the stirrup, facing the audience. Hunching forward, she tightened the helmet and flicked her riding crop behind her with a neat turn of the wrist.

"They're off," called Sam. "Take it off, take it off," sang out Carney, grabbing three more cups of beer from the speedy waiter. The band sounded "The Lone Ranger" theme, and some called, "They're off!"

Celeste smiled and simulated riding while unbuttoning her vest. When it fell open, the customers saw her bare breasts, tight and high but bouncing as she pretended to race.

258

The twins were howling, and, despite himself, Oscar felt excited. He wouldn't want to be seen by any of the girls he knew. But then again, none of the girls he knew was here!

Celeste dismounted, threw away her helmet and vest, and pranced about the stage. Almost by magic she stepped out of her shoes, then wiggled her hips so she could push down her jodhpurs. She had on only a G-string.

"Now you'll see, now you'll see!" shouted Carney.

Oscar was dry mouthed.

In one swift move, Celeste spun the sawhorse 180 degrees and mounted it with her back to the audience. As she rode to the finish, her bottom elevated and rocking, Oscar understood why she was called "The Celestial Fanny."

Then he wondered: who had the more divine behind, Janet Middleton or Mattie Hill?

When the boys had no more money to pay for drink and to (try to) tip the dancers, they staggered out to the car. Oscar talked Sam into letting him take the wheel and gingerly eased the DeSoto out of the mud beside the road. He didn't want to get stuck, be rescued, and then have to explain to his mother how the three of them had ended up at the Sink Hole.

Having descended to their level for a night himself, he decided he should not get on a high horse (he chuckling to himself at the pun) and lecture his cousins about their behavior. In fact, as he drove, he did a lot of thinking about the Celestial Fanny on a wooden charger.

Like many others, he had been mesmerized watching a news reel account of Seabiscuit beating Triple Crown winner Admiral (son of Man o' War) in a thrilling special race at Pimlico Race Course. And as they came into the stretch, Oscar saw on film the jockeys' raised rumps rise and fall with the horses' gaits. What he'd witnessed tonight was something different and related more to the bedroom than to the racetrack.

Most of the accounts of lovemaking he'd read focused on the powerful actions of the man. The woman, if described in any detail, was generally passive, receiving the energy of her lover. But Celeste's hip movements, clearly suggesting more than an equestrian application, had their own force. In addition to up and down above her imaginary steed there was an energetic forward and backward pelvic driving that stuck in Oscar's mind.

The next day he took an extra Ridgetop menu and left it for Mattie at The Towers, with a note that he often had lunch at the cafe. And for the rest of the week, he made sure to be around through the middle of the day.

"I can help clear dishes, if you'd like," he told his aunt one day. "I don't want to take up a stool when business is brisk." He was sitting at the end of the counter, a place most customers seemed to avoid when there were other choices.

"If there's no seat left, I'll let you know. You keep studying."

Oscar had told her he found the cafe a convenient place to prepare for his last year of college by reading textbooks; and on some days he did puzzle over an introduction to advanced astronomy. But at this moment he was studying a newspaper story about a planned movie adaptation of John Steinbeck's *The Grapes of Wrath*.

It brought to mind his Uncle Edgar telling him about families who'd abandoned farms in southwestern Missouri and across Oklahoma. Drought, dust-storms, and hard times had driven farmers west in search of opportunity. Up until then, Oscar had thought of Steinbeck's novel in terms of its artistic successes and shortcomings, not so much as a reflection of real people.

"Our minister's sister's family down in Fidelity," Uncle Edgar said, "they had to pack up and leave with nothing that wouldn't fit in their pick-up truck. The bank swooped in and took all that was left. I suspect they made a handsome bit of money selling that stuff and the land."

"Who would buy the farm," Oscar asked, "if it wasn't worth working anymore?" Aunt Irene and her daughters were cleaning up in the kitchen while the men sat out on the front porch. Sam and Carney were whittling and, as usual, not paying much attention to their father.

"That's the thing. There was oil down there, but Missy didn't know it. No one did, except some gas company people. They'd had their geologists snooping around there for a few years, doing tests and taking measurements. They knew the surface land was shot, but deep down below were hidden riches."

Although a city dweller now, Uncle Edgar still smoked his corn cob pipe, stereotypical recreation of an Ozark farmer. At the request of his wife, however, he did so only at home. He loaded, lit, and drew on it almost unconsciously. He also blew perfect smoke rings that rose, stayed together, and floated gracefully across the porch if--as it was now--the breeze were light.

"Did the family, your friends, do better in another place?"

262

Edgar tamped down the tobacco in his pipe with the flap of a matchbook and then drew the flame into it with long breaths. "That's the thing. They did and they didn't."

Oscar raised his eyebrows.

"You see, they had a daughter who ended up in Hollywood. Had real talent, a singer. At first, of course, she went for audition after audition; got nowhere."

Oscar thought of Shirley Temple in *Little Miss Broadway,* one of the many popular rags-to-riches movies of the time. An orphan is brought to a failing boarding house for actors and actresses. The little girl's talent and enthusiasm lead her and Pop Shea, her parents' friend who has taken her in, to fame and fortune in the big city.

"But she was good, you say?"

"Yes. And one day she . . . um, found the right producer. She got paid big money to perform, and that saved the family."

"I have a feeling there's more to the story."

Uncle Edgar blew a series of thoughtful smoke rings. "Yes, yes, there is. Her family never knew where she was working, but it turns out Little Marilyn was singing for a burlesque house, before the dancers came on. Well, the strippers."

"Ah."

"And eventually they wanted her to join the other girls. They gave her the choice of that or nothing."

"That's tough. The way of the world, I guess. So, what happened?"

"You know, Oscar, I think I'm not going to say what became of her, except that she was able to give her family enough money to start over. And then she sort of . . . disappeared."

Oscar wondered if the Celestial Fanny could sing. Or if she had a family she'd left behind somewhere. "Perhaps she saved enough to start over in another life, with a different name, in a . . . more respectable establishment."

"Let's believe that's what happened."

Oscar thought for a few moments. "Did she, the girl, have a special song for auditions?"

"Interesting that you should ask." He realized his pipe had gone out, inspected it, then rapped it on the edge of an ashtray until it was empty. "It was 'Moonglow.'"

Sitting at the counter in the Ridgetop and reading the article about a possible movie version of The *Grapes of Wrath*, Oscar recalled this conversation with his uncle. He heard the lyrics from "*Moonglow*"--"Heavenly songs . . . way up in the blue"--and concluded that the girl who sang about the moon had been cruelly brought down to earth.

Her story reminded him that there was to be a song-writing contest next fall at Wesleyan. He would be entering into a competition pretty soon himself. He knew the $100.00 prize could help the family finances and was confident he had the ability to win.

Back in Salinas he had even sketched out a melody. Thinking of "*Moonglow*" now inspired a possible verse: "Angel of love, / You are my theme. / Hover above, / You are my dream." He pulled out a little pocket notebook and jotted down the words.

Staring out across the lunch crowd in his aunt's cafe, he decided the song's beloved needed a more specific identity. At the same time, the figure had to be general enough that listeners/judges would pour their own fantasies into the outline he provided. He imagined a talented young girl traveling to Los Angeles or New York, knowing her family depends on her to make it big. The song could be about a girl who aspired to stardom.

He pursued the idea. Rather than a heartless producer who would exploit her innocence, this girl could meet a successful movie scriptwriter. A kind man, who was also a talented horn player, he would suggest that they work together on an album.

He lived in a marvelous house on a large estate. Its vertical structure lifted one up from gritty realities that spoiled dreams. Always proper, he showed her its features, including a small recording studio built off the library. Moved by her story of past hardship, he would propose a partnership: he was to compose and she was to sing: "Journeying high, / You are my dream. / Above a sigh, / You are my theme."

Although their relationship had begun as a business arrangement, over time he would come to realize that he loved this simple, trusting girl. She, of course, had loved him at first sight.

Still, she would know he had been a man about town who could drink his friends under the table or put his foes there with his fists. He'd played in nightclubs and visited other less reputable places of entertainment. But she knew he was a good man at heart. She had dreamed of him, and now he was hers.

"There's a woman who needs a seat, Oscar," he heard his Aunt Agnes say. And he turned around up to see Mattie Hill smiling at him from the doorway.

Oscar jumped up immediately and waved her to his seat at the counter. As she settled herself there, he saw that she had the menu he'd left for her. He was also struck again by her dark-complexioned, exotic beauty.

"Hi, Oscar," she said. "Thanks for dropping this off for me. As you can see, I've come to try the fare. What do you recommend?"

"The ham salad is my favorite, but, of course," he said smiling, "everything's good here--family restaurant, you see."

"Ha-ha! Well, Missouri raises its share of hogs. But . . . " She turned to Aunt Agnes, who was on the other side of the counter holding her order tablet, "make mine the chicken salad."

Oscar had stepped to the end of the counter but knew he would have to get out of the way of the staff passing to and from the kitchen. His aunt, however, a good reader of customers and nephews, took him by the elbow. "We can get by easier if you'll sit here." A stool had opened up on the other side of Mattie.

He was happy to comply and said to Mattie, "Just in case it doesn't turn out, I'll keep you company . . . if that's okay."

"Sure. You can tell me how your group--Undertones?--is doing. Are you looking for other places to play?"

"Maybe. I don't know how long I'll be here. My mother and I are really just visiting while my father is in Sweden. He, um, went on family business."

"Ah. So, you'll go back to . . . ?"

"Salinas, Kansas. Yes, I'll begin my last year of college in September. Then it's on to advanced study at . . . a university." He wanted to say Harvard or Chicago but realized that such a statement, even if true, might be what his mother termed "uppity."

Her lunch plate arrived, and Mattie put the napkin over her lap. "It looks delicious."

Oscar thought she'd pick up her knife and fork and eat immediately. But she lowered her head a moment and looked down thoughtfully. He was about to ask if there was something wrong when he realized she was saying a silent grace. He looked down himself for a moment.

She raised her head and asked, "But you're in town rescuing fair damsels in distress for a few weeks at least, perhaps the summer?"

Oscar feared blood was rushing to his face, so he answered quickly. "That's right. It's a nice change of pace." He wanted to ask about the night he had rescued her--whom she had been with, why she was singled out by the drunken customer.

"You are in a state capitol, so it might be more exciting here. Ooh, that's good!" She'd taken a bite of the chicken salad.

"So far it's been pretty similar to Salinas. I haven't seen many sights, though, because my mother's brothers are here and we're doing a lot of family visiting." He omitted his trip to the Sink Hole from his list of experiences.

"That's nice. You can always count on family."

"Is your family here, in Jefferson City?"

"No. Chicago, actually. I came here because of the job. It was a big step up for me."

"Hmm. How did you get into politics, and so far from home? If you don't mind my asking."

"Not at all. I've been inspired by the President's wife, Eleanor Roosevelt. I read her column, 'My Day.' I always find it so uplifting!"

Most of Oscar's friends and relatives disliked Roosevelt and his policies, which, they felt, undermined the importance of self-reliance. They also feared he would be persuaded to lead the country into war. Their distrust extended to Mrs. Roosevelt, whose activism was even more offensive because she was a woman.

"I'm afraid I've never been terribly interested in government, but I do wonder what it's like in

269

the halls of power as opposed to the ivory tower of academe."

"Ha! It's more boring than you can imagine . . . at least, most of the time." A worried look he'd seen before passed over her face.

"Is it that way right now? You seemed to say the other day that it can be a very competitive arena. Do the best come to the top or the . . . most ruthless?"

Mattie had finished her meal and turned down Aunt Agnes' suggestion of apple pie for dessert. She turned to look at him. "I didn't think it ruthless when I was your age. I was innocent, perhaps because of a sheltered childhood."

Another group of customers had come in the cafe, and Oscar knew he should leave. But he didn't want to end this conversation. "Why don't we go outside? We could walk over to the capitol grounds and sit on a bench for awhile, before you have to go back to work."

"It might do me good to hear about college in Kansas, so long as you don't tell of being whisked up and away to Oz by a tornado!"

Oscar promised not to. In fact, he didn't like that movie, already enormously popular. He could not see the Lion, the Tin Man, or the Scarecrow as proper heroes. The wizard losing control of his own balloon seemed the final blow to the notion that a great man would have broken through all the fakery of this land. And in the end it was all a silly girl's dream anyway.

270

He told Mattie about his hopes to be an architect . . . or a scientist or a poet or a genius inventor. He was pleased to see her smile at his enthusiasm.

When he'd reached a temporary stopping point in his projections, she said, "So you will rise from humble beginnings to great importance, but not as a leader of the people."

He laughed. "Oh, I don't know. The people might come ask me to step up on the throne, after I've accomplished so much and received all sorts of recognition."

"You don't lack ambition! But, if you do, I could be your spokesperson. I'm getting all this on-the-job training right now."

"Didn't you study government in college?"

"Oh, no. I majored in social work, committed to the causes of justice and public welfare." It seemed as if she were quoting from the college catalog.

Again, Oscar's vague political leanings allied such a program with a lack of belief in individual initiative and resourcefulness. "What made you choose that?"

"I'm the child of a . . . minister, so I guess it came naturally."

"I see. My uncle, the father of two of the other boys in Undertones, is a minister."

"Really! You know, when I was younger, I thought about becoming a preacher myself. But that's not considered a proper role for a woman."

Oscar thought of Dinah Morris in George Eliot's novel, *Adam Bede*. She had no recognized place in a church but preached in the fields to ordinary folks. She also possessed a quality that drew others to her. Knowing that Eliot (well, Marian Evans, who wrote under that pen name) was a skeptic, he admired the force of her fictional character.

He'd once seen a silent film of the novel, made several decades earlier. In an odd way, the fact that the movie Dinah's words could not be heard increased his interest in her. Perhaps he gave the screen character the voice of someone he knew. Or he could have imagined her having the speech of angels.

"Women can be important in politics, like the President's wife. And they say a good secretary often runs the important offices."

She laughed and shook her head. "Perhaps that's so, but so far I do all the running for the men in my job." She looked at her watch. "And I need to get back to running!"

They stood up, but she didn't start walking immediately, as if giving him a chance to say something. So he did. "I'd like to see you again. Maybe you could show me the important places in the city, where decisions are made and deals struck."

272

"Hmm. I might be able to do even more. Would you be free to take a day-trip with me out of town this weekend?"

"Sure. I mean, would this be business or pleasure?"

"Some of both. There's a project under consideration by the governor's office involving land down south of here. Actually, it's a mountain that's supposed to be very picturesque. But it's not easy to get to. That's why you could help me, in case of flat tires or something."

"That would be swell! A chance to see the countryside."

He couldn't have known at the time that the outing with Mattie would be memorable not just for what he learned on Sorrel Bluff but also for what he found out when he returned.

For the rest of the week, Oscar felt he was just marking time until he could go off on an adventure with the governor's assistant. However, he knew he had first to present this outing to his mother as a proper and official event. It turned out that the fabrication he came up need not have been so elaborate. Sallie, preoccupied about her absent husband, was not concerned abut his plans..

"Aunt Kristina sent me a newspaper story--flooding in southern Sweden. Bridges have been washed out, and whole houses swept downstream. I'm so worried about Carl!"

"Now mother, you're just working yourself up for nothing. He's probably already on his way home. Why, I bet a postcard will come soon indicating when he's to arrive." They were in the kitchen, Sallie helping her mother make pickles. Grandpa had brought the cucumbers in from the small garden plot in their side yard.

"Would you go into the pantry and get more canning jars down from the top shelf? I don't want to slip off the stool and get hurt. Why, then both of your parents would be incapacitated!"

Oscar glanced at Grandma, who, having entered that stage of life in which more and more friends and family members were being taken from her, showed no alarm. Oscar could reach the jars without the stepping stool, but he struggled to figure out how he could ease his mother's fears. "How many do you need?" he called out.

"Half a dozen will do. Just make sure each one has a good lid."

Oscar looked out the screen door across the backyard toward downtown. He could see the capitol building perched on the high ridge. And he imagined Mattie perched on the edge of the governor's desk, notebook in hand and pencil behind an ear. "Do I give them the go-ahead, sir, or do I say you're still consulting the parties to be affected?"

"Here you are, Mother. Oh, did I tell you I'm going on a little excursion Saturday?"

"Not with . . . " He knew she wanted to say "with Sam and Carney" but was observing her private rules of discretion. "Not with anyone I would disapprove of, I hope."

"I'm sure you wouldn't. I've been asked to accompany a party from the governor's office. It's an inspection of a site where they might be building a celestial observatory."

"And you were asked? My, but you've met important people quickly here!"

"Just one of the staff. It was at Aunt Agnes', where a lot of government workers eat."

"And they snapped you up to do their work for them?"

She was dropping cucumber slices into jars and pouring hot pickling juice over them. Grandmother put a lid in place and screwed down the cap as mechanically as a machine.

"No, no. I won't be doing anyone's work. They thought I might be a good observer; and I get to ride along for free. You see, I was studying my astronomy textbook, and an aide asked me if I knew how to use parallax and the standard candle index to calculate the distance between heavenly bodies. We got to talking, and one thing led to another."

He figured she wouldn't understand if he clouded his explanation with scientific concepts. Sallie nodded. "That makes sense. You know so much about everything, Oscar. Where will this expedition take you?"

"Out to a hilltop in the country south of here. The air is clearer there, and the higher you are, the thinner the atmosphere. You can see better through telescopes."

"I suppose it might be good for your career to be asked to go on a scientific expedition."

"That's . . . that's what I thought. You can't learn everything in textbooks." He chuckled to himself, remembering how inadequate his understanding of lovemaking, based on reading novels and medical books, had been. "Practical experience is always good."

"Do you need me to pack a lunch, then? Or will the governor be supplying everything you need?"

"Why, Mother, any lunch you make will be better than what the state provides! Say, make enough for two. There's another young person going as an observer, and we could share."

Oscar left his grandparents' house that Saturday morning with a basket full of cucumber sandwiches, deviled eggs, and cookies. He was to meet Mattie on the capitol steps, confident he was not going to be whisked off to Shangri-La like Conway in *Lost Horizons*.

Oscar had bought the new paperback edition of that novel, having already read the college library edition a number of times. The idea of being transported to another land and recognized as a spiritual leader appealed to him. In the Shangri-La scenario he created for himself, he would also win a number of fights before his elevation to high priest. And, of course, there would a harpsichord-playing Lo-Tsen with whom he would make beautiful music.

Standing on Sorrel Bluff looking down at the Niangua River that afternoon, he felt Mattie was as beautiful as any foreign princess. And the landscape, though not the Himalayas, was impressive. "They say an Indian maiden threw herself down to the rocks below," she explained, "rather than marry a man she didn't love."

They were an hour and a half southwest of Jefferson City in an area that was changing rapidly after the creation of the Osage Reservoir. Construction of the Bagnell Dam and a hydroelectric plant brought jobs to the depressed area. But the explosion of recreational facilities along the lake's 1,000-mile shoreline would forever alter the nature of little rural communities.

"It's a beautiful place," Oscar said. "A bit more hilly than in Kansas!"

She laughed. "Yes, I suppose so." She looked back down the wooded path they had climbed to reach this point and chewed her lip. "There are more places one might slip and fall."

"I have a feeling you mean that metaphorically as well as literally."

"Yes, I suppose I do. You see, there's a family--a wealthy family--that owns a lot of land around here. They want to build a resort hotel down on the river, which has become a lake now that the dam is finished. They'll have a cam train running up the bluff to this spot--Lovers' Leap."

He had put the basket down beside a large rock. Now he started laying the food out. "Okay, but how is the governor's office involved?" She sat beside him.

"The locals down here . . . they're not so keen on progress. They want to just keep farming and living the way they always have. So, the Yardlys, who helped the governor get into office, want the state to wade in, put some pressure on county officials."

"Ah. Well, there would be opportunities here, I guess--jobs in hard times."

"True, but many feel a way of life will be lost. I told you I'm from Chicago, but really I grew up in a little town outside of the big city and I understand. Ours is a tight community, with churches and synagogues keeping people together, helping when there's need." She took a bite of a sandwich and smiled, either at the memory or the sandwich.

"Crowds of fun-loving tourists might not be the best thing, even if they bring money."

"From what I learned doing research about other places like this, a lot of the locals end up moving away, trying to recreate what they had somewhere else."

"And I bet some people have already seen their farms go under water as the river rose."

"Yes." She paused and then turned to him. "Oscar, I asked you to come along today so I could get your views on this. You're . . . young, fresh, forward looking. If I go along, am I in danger of compromising my principles?"

He chafed at the role she was asking him to play. He was more a man of the world than she knew. "Politics can be a dirty game. We all know that. But the good people have to stay in the fight, stand up for the little guy. That's what you'd be doing."

She sighed. "I have to admit, though, there are rewards for me, temptations. If I persuade the governor's deputy on tourism to get involved, it'll mean a big promotion. I might be able to do more good later in a new position. You know, control the shape of future growth."

"Lose the battle but win the war."

"Exactly. I please the Yardlys and they continue to help the governor. Change comes, but we manage it for good." She stood up. "Of course, there is one more item. The deputy . . . he, ah, wants something in return for his cooperation."

He was folding the napkins and putting them back in the basket. "Oh?"

She looked again down to the river. "Yes. He wants me to sit on his lap."

"Well, that's a bit odd, but not so bad."

She gave him a crooked smile. "With no clothes on?"

Oscar was so shocked at the proposal--and her apparent willingness even to consider it--that the logical conclusion from what she had said didn't come to him until they were back in the car and on the way home: the governor's deputy on tourism must be the man he'd floored at Eddie's Basement!

"Your father has been hurt, just as I said he would be," Oscar's mother announced, handing him a telegraph when he entered the living room of his grandparents' house. His hand shook as he read the communiqué from his father's cousin.

In a moment he looked up. "But he's okay, Mother. Yes, his leg is badly broken, and it will take time. But they say that they were able to set the bones and he can expect a full recovery." Her stoic look told him she was ready to face the hardship that had come to them; but he also foresaw that her resentment would be deep and long-lasting.

A failed latch at the Malmo train station was the cause of Carl's injury, not the violent winds or rampaging rivers Sallie had feared. A wagonload of wooden crates tumbled onto him as he was descending a long stairway. He heard it coming only in time to turn and be rolled down the last steps in an avalanche of splintering pine.

"We must prepare for his coming back," his mother said, "But he will need to be taken care of for months, maybe longer. Oh, Oscar, how will we get on? He can't work. We've wasted what little savings we'd been able to put aside on this trip."

His grandparents, who were sitting with Sallie, expressed their concern; but Oscar knew they could offer no remedy other than seeking God's will. And this was advice that had always irritated him. Shouldn't we fight to succeed rather than submit to some plan hatched by a god whose existence was unproven?

They all expected that Carl would be bedridden for some time and only gradually recover the ability to walk and take care of himself. They couldn't afford a convalescence home, so he and his mother would have to devote themselves to his care.

Even as they talked and worried, Oscar thought of Irene Dunne in *Love Affair*. A singer is engaged to one man falls in love with another (Charles Boyer). Tragically struck by a car, she is presumed crippled for the rest of her life; so she breaks a promise to meet her new lover at the top of the Empire State Building, not wanting to be a burden.

Oscar loved that the couple chose the highest building in the world's biggest city for their rendezvous. And he admired a woman who would not hold back the man she loved, an artist whose work, Oscar believed, would ease the suffering and raise the spirits of many.

Oscar could only think of himself escaping disasters, not succumbing to them. The trajectory of the future was to begin with a college degree (and related honors, of course), and that had to be paid for by . . . well, now it would have to be funded by a miracle.

Even though his father had been hurt fulfilling a request of his brothers and sisters, Oscar couldn't count on them to provide for his parents and raise money for him to finish college. And he couldn't work enough hours after school to meet such expenses.

"Mother, we'll find a way. Right now we need to be thankful that he's coming home. We must get back to Salinas and make arrangements. You know how strong he is. Why, this won't be worse for him than being on his hands and knees dragging coal out of the mines."

Oscar also recalled his father's revelation about his time in the Swedish army. Rather than facing physical hardships, he had had to overcome guilt for shooting down men he couldn't think of as his enemies. With all that he'd encountered, Carl was steadfast.

"Well, we will see. Right now I must write to Aunt Kristina and ask her to get our little house ready for our return. You'll need to tell others-- your cousins, the boss at the movie theater--that you'll be gone by . . . the end of the month, I guess."

The only person in Jefferson City he particularly wanted to see again was Mattie, though what he would ask or say to her after her revelation was uncertain. She had agreed to go with him to the movies on Friday, but he certainly couldn't pursue romance with her in the way he had intended. The image of her, a minister's daughter, with a man's hand up her dress blurred in his mind with a picture of her sitting on the same man's lap. He was unsure of his role with such a woman.

He thought again of *Love Affair*, of how Charles Boyer immediately committed himself to Irene Dunne despite her paralysis. In the projection Oscar wrote in his head for that couple's future, she discovered not only that she could walk again, but that her singing voice had somehow improved through her trauma. And, later, as her husband, Charles Boyer would have his work accepted by the most prestigious galleries throughout Europe.

What he needed to do, Oscar soon decided, was talk with his Aunt Agnes. She had survived caring for an invalid; and she had been his confidant on matters of love. He wanted to know where she looked for strength in facing the future. When he stopped by the Ridgetop cafe the next day, however, she turned the question back to him.

"Oscar," she said after hearing that Sallie planned to leave in a few weeks for Kansas, "I have a story to tell you." She had just been next door to check on her husband. The cafe was closed and the staff were preparing for tomorrow's business.

"I hope it has a hero who overcomes many obstacles to realize his dreams."

"It's about a girl who learns to endure. Here: help me with the salt shakers." She had brought the several dozen standard glass containers to a booth and was unscrewing the caps.

He took the Morton carton and began filling. The large container and the little opening made it hard not to spill, so it was slow work.

"Do you remember my telling you that I planned to be an artist once?"

"Yes, before you married Uncle John."

"Your mother was just a girl then, still living on the farm. She worshipped her older brother. In fact, I think she was a bit jealous of me for taking him away."

"She can be . . . a bit possessive."

"Anyway, I was studying sculpture that fall at a little studio only a few blocks from here. We had a difficult assignment: to design something that drew the viewer into the piece."

Oscar was studying the iconic Morton salt girl pictured on the box, She seemed too happy for the rain that was coming down on her umbrella. How could she smile when her little shoes were obviously getting soaked?

He asked his aunt, "You mean the work had to involve others in whatever it represented?"

"Not just that. It had to pull them into the material itself, into the glass or stone or wood."

"That's a challenge. Why was that important?"

"My teacher said art sometimes stands apart from life, giving us a fanciful world where we escape our troubles and our responsibilities. But he believed art must involve us with complexity and inspire us to return to life with new energy and commitment."

"Ah, so you made a tar baby!" Oscar's mother had read him the Uncle Remus stories when he was younger; and he later reread this particular piece in *Harper's Weekly*, where it had appeared. The story always irritated him. Surely, you could free yourself from a lump of tar!

"Not exactly, but the idea might be similar. I made the lair of a trapdoor spider."

"The guy that puts a lid over his burrow and pops out to catch unsuspecting prey?"

"Right. The spider hinges the door, a combination of dirt and silk and plant material, on one side, so it also snaps back into place to protect him."

"Although there are some predators that get in and sting them. The venom doesn't kill them, but the eggs they lay nearby hatch into larvae that eat them alive. Not a happy fate."

He looked again at the Morton girl, whose happiness, he guessed, was to be shared by customers. As the slogan declared, "When it rains, it pours"; that is, their salt would never clump up. But the skipping girl's satisfaction seemed unjustified because she didn't realize salt was spilling out of the box she carried. Oscar wanted her to stay out of the rain in the first place.

"Yes, there's another side to every story! I made a very large trapdoor spider burrow. It might have been two feet across. And the hole was deep, spiraling down into a tiny space."

"And the spider was hiding in there, ready to leap out?"

"No. That's what everyone thought, and they'd peer through the slit. The door was only open a little, so it wasn't easy to see. But I'd designed it so that viewers would want to look."

"Okay, so what did they see?"

"At the bottom was a little disk of special, metallic clay, polished to a beautiful shine."

"Ah, so a mirror! What was it someone said about Jekyll in Stevenson's novel?--'the mere radiance of a foul soul that thus transpires through, and transfigures, its clay continent?'"

"I don't know about that, Oscar. But I do believe to overcome obstacles--and to find your soul mate--I know that you must look within, not outside, for answers."

"There will be no hero on a white horse riding to my rescue?"

She looked hard at him and then gave her enigmatic answer. "Only one."

A second telegram from Carl's cousin arrived the following week, giving more grim news. It seemed that, once he was back in the United States, Oscar's father would need a second operation. If his recovery continued as hoped, though, he would be on a ship to New York in a fortnight. From there he would come by train to Kansas City, where they could meet him.

Oscar understood, then, that his mother's role as nurse--and his as her assistant--would not begin for at least a month. But he also began to see how long his father's convalescence might be. Unless something intervened, it appeared increasingly unlikely he would be able to return to school in September; instead he would have to find some sort of employment.

There was a last resort he hoped to avoid: his Uncle Nils was offering to take him on as an apprentice carpenter. It wouldn't pay much even if there were contractors who needed them, but he could also work on the farm for food if business was slow.

His parents had always assumed he would rise above working with his hands, the next generation moving up the social ladder. And that idea had been so intertwined with his own vision of the future that digging in the earth or hammering nails into a floor would mean slipping to the level of his ancestors--a failure of the American dream.

He wrote to his friend Bob, alerting him of his predicament and asking him to keep an ear open for any possibilities of work. He also sent a somewhat maudlin note to Janet Middleton, which was too obviously a bid for sympathy.

"As you go back to the campus, with the leaves turning golden and the harvests complete, don't forget your one-time physics lab partner, who will be conducting live experiments on the force needed to shovel cow manure from barn floor to wagon bed to yard heaps, the volume of excrement produced versus the bales of hay consumed, the amount of heat generated by a man's decaying hopes." He couldn't have guessed that his sentimental posing would contribute toward an unexpected boon; but, indirectly, it did.

In the meantime, the movie date with Mattie Hill grew in his mind as one last chance to carry the joy of summer romance into a season of discontent. He recalled a previous escape from the ordinary, the weekend trip to St. Louis when he was in high school. There he'd toured a big city and encountered a woman from the even bigger city of New York.

Miss Lacy's face had sunk out of his memory for a time, but then rose again as, waiting to escort Janet to the dance at St. Mary's a few months ago, he had gazed off into the sunset.

Mingled with the varied reds of a prairie sky at dusk, her image hovered in the air, an inspiration. He wanted to take another haunting memory from his meeting with Mattie.

As Friday approached, however, Oscar occasionally felt a dip in confidence. After all, she worked at the top of the state's power structure, and his honors were yet to be earned. He considered concocting reasons not to go--his mother had a high fever, he had to clean out his grandparents' attic, the creeks would rise. But Mattie was pretty. And his ego needed that romantic moment.

At The Towers he watched the numbers record the elevator's descent. Hmm, she lived on the top floor--the penthouse? She stepped through the doors wearing an attractive, dark business outfit and asked if he could step in for a few moments.

As they crossed the foyer, he admitted that he had some bad news. "I have to go back to Kansas in a few weeks. My father's been in an accident on his travels, and my mother and I have to be ready to take care of him when he returns."

"Oh, dear! But he'll recover?"

She had led him into a reception area off the lobby, a circular room with a sunken floor rimmed by dark wood furniture. A number of small lamps hanging from the ceiling and pottery set on posts made the room seem oddly like a cave with stalagmites and stalactites. He hoped bats weren't ready to descend from the shadows above his head! This certainly didn't suit Oscar's architectural preferences.

"Yes," he said about his father's recovery. "At least that's what his cousin writes. He's going to need more surgery."

"Will this affect your going back to school?"

"I'm afraid so. But right now I'm unhappy it affects my chances to . . . to get to know you better."

She smiled. "That's a nice thing to say! I was looking forward to your being in town a bit longer, too. You're good to talk to, someone who listens to my troubles."

"Ah, yes, your . . . choices. The resort hotel and new business but at a cost."

She frowned, and he realized that it would have been better not to spell out the difficult options she faced. "Say," he said, looking at his watch. "We should watch the time. *The Man in the Iron Mask* starts in thirty minutes, and we have a fifteen-minute walk to get there."

"I walk fast. And, well, there was something I wanted to say, too." She opened the newspaper she had tucked under her arm. "You follow the news?"

"In a general way, I guess. Something specific?"

"Specific but widespread. It makes my personal worries seem insignificant."

"The world is always in turmoil. I try not to let it bother me."

"I understand, but there are times when you can't keep it away. Have you ever heard of an 'Office for Jewish Emigration'?"

"No. Is it part of the Missouri government?"

"No. It's not local, not even in this country. One has been set up in Vienna. And there is talk across Europe of other, similar offices being planned for Prague and Berlin. Do you know what 'emigration'--or, 'Auswanderung'--means in this case?"

"'Ous-von . . . ?' I would guess they're traveling from Europe to Palestine, that region."

"I wish that were so, but more and more we think there's a plan to remove us from . . . from the earth."

This was so fantastic an assertion that he couldn't take it in. Then, he replayed her statement in his head. "'Us?'" he asked.

"I'm a Jew, Oscar. These are my people."

"I see. Yes, I thought that was . . . the case."

All he could think of was Rebecca in Sir Walter Scott's *Ivanhoe*, lovely daughter of a medieval moneylender and skilled healer. He also knew about the historical Rebecca Gratz, a beautiful Hebrew friend of Washington Irving and possible inspiration for Scott's character. Both women were unwilling to marry men outside their faith. He'd never met a Jew himself until now.

"One of the things I liked about you, Oscar, was that you didn't treat me any differently than anyone else. You're a . . . a regular American, but you didn't put me in a special category. So it was good to hear your advice about politics . . . and other things."

How much she understood of his true thoughts, Oscar could not say. His knowledge of Jews and their place in America was unformed, vaguely in tune with a common feeling that they were outsiders, that they had influence, that there was nothing wrong with restricting their rights.

Mattie told him that she would be resigning her position in Jefferson City soon and returning to Chicago. She was going to work for an organization that publicized the plight of Jews in Europe. Both she and he, it seemed, were being pulled away by family obligations.

Still, agreeing to delay taking on their family obligations for one night at least, they went to see Joan Bennet as Princess Maria Theresa of Spain and Louis Hayward as the man in the iron mask (and his twin). Oscar, having devoured all the Dumas books he could find, identified with d'Artagnan, played by Warren William, who rescues the prince and saves a country.

Oscar's real life worries about his own future did not end soon, but a godsend was waiting from Dr. Bohns when he returned home. He was offered a one-year, full-time position as the professor's assistant. He would receive a salary he couldn't expect to earn elsewhere. His formal studies would have to be postponed, but he would be learning some sophisticated research techniques. He would become, for the time being, the breadwinner for the family.

He was even more pleased to learn that he owed his nomination for the position to Janet Middleton, his rival in academic achievement and a continuing love interest. Though she would not be the woman he married--his soulmate was, in fact, at this time thousands of miles away-- together they learned much in the next year about mathematics and desire.

Oscar had to accept a pause in the rise to distinction his parents had always expected; but the interruption of that ascent may have nurtured strength and a sense of purpose that made his later accomplishments more lasting. At least, that's what he came to believe in time.

Epilogue: Clock Hands

"I hope that's a toy for one of the grandchildren," I told Curtis when I saw the contraption on the dining room table. I was walking (with the cane my children require me to use now) down the hall from the first-floor guest room toward the family room, where the party for me would be held the next day.

"That? Why, it could be for your 97th birthday, Nana. You'll be clocking many more hours, days, and years in the future."

"So it is a clock?" What I saw was a rectangular solid (the size of the old standard, a breadbox) made of glass or, more likely, plastic. Inside a zigzag series of chutes went from top to bottom.

"It's a rolling ball clock, inspired by the Congreve model from the early 19th century. Want to know how it works?"

I knew I had no choice, but I've always appreciated his enthusiasm for mechanical things, especially when they are also historical artifacts. As a scholar of the Victorian period, he enjoys explaining how that generation lived and thought.

"See, here at the bottom is a reservoir of metal balls. Every second this little arm," he pointed," swings down and the bucket at the end picks up one ball. It lifts it up here," another gesture, "and drops it into the top rail."

"It's not running now, though, right?"

"Right. I haven't put the batteries in yet."

"Wait a minute! You have a mechanical clock that needs batteries?"

"It's a representation of how the original ones worked, Nana. Don't be critical."

As he talked, he pulled off the top, inserted six batteries in the body, and reassembled the clock. "For his time machine, Congreve constructed a tilting table with a long zigzag groove for the ball to roll down. When the ball reached the end of the track, its weight tipped the table, and the ball went back the other way."

"Ah. So, the rocking table was like a pendulum in a grandfather clock."

He pushed a switch, and the little arm swept down to get a ball, lift it up, and drop it. "Well, sort of. But for me to build one would take a lot of time I don't have right now, given all the writing you have me doing. So I decided to enjoy this."

I saw the ball in Curtis' contraption reach the bottom and a dial advance to register the tick or tock of time's passing. "Well, I'll tell you what this reminds me of: the visible escalator system back in a Jefferson City hotel your father liked so much."

"Yes, the one you told me about that revealed there is only one structure--not separate up and down escalators. The motor just turns the drive wheels one way or other."

"Ah, you remember! Oscar loved to watch its connected system at work until . . . well, at least until it came to remind him of the two-year delay in his college career."

"Two-year? I thought he had to take care of his father for one fall, a year at most."

"It did take a year for his father to return to work, but even then not at the pace he'd been able to manage before. And then Grandma had another breakdown. Fortunately, Oscar's position as Dr. Bohn's assistant was continued a second year, but he felt he fell behind another year."

"Hmm. He had to take care of his parents for two years? He never told me that."

"He resented that interruption in his education so much he almost never spoke of it. But, because he was really two years younger than his fellow students when he graduated from high school, he finished college at the same age as his classmates."

"Maybe that's why I never thought about it. I knew the year he was born, so the time frame after that made sense."

"And you are a man who wants an orderly sequence of events."

Curtis studied and wrote about the Victorian serial novel, which was published as regularly as a clock, once a week or a month. He believes this tick-tock structure matched others in the first industrial age: train travel, factory production, academic calendar, the church year.

"I always have liked regularity, part of my Midwestern cultural assimilation."

"For your father, it was as if he had become the escalator, not the passenger. He went up and then back down, forward now and backward next, while his classmates, like Janet Middleton, moved in one direction through time."

"I can see how that would have been frustrating. It was also a time when the world seemed to go forward and backwards, wasn't it?"

"Yes, on in scientific progress but back to war and destruction. And your father worried that the latter would affect his future if he ever got back on track."

"When did the draft start? As I remember, he was turned down at first."

"He was--poor eyesight. Let's see, 1940 I think was the draft, but it operated on a lottery system before Pearl Harbor in 1941. And men served twelve months, not 'for the duration,' as would be the case before long."

"And by then Dad was working for the Navy?"

"Yes, doing who knows what, but it involved weapons research."

"The bomb?"

"Not directly, I think, but . . . who knows? Oscar was a believer in security and was careful even in his talks with me: 'Loose lips sink ships.' I do know the military wanted him in the lab, not on a battlefield."

"Things changed for my generation. Whatever your skills, if they needed infantry when your name came up, infantry you were."

Curtis knows he was lucky that, after being drafted, the Army made him a correspondent. He had equally well-trained friends who found themselves in the jungle.

"I think more people joined up in our era," I explained. "And it seemed as if we were losing them every day." I was thinking of my first love, Tony Giordano, killed in Africa. "Your father's music teacher, Professor Lewis, died while training. Two of his cousins were lost in the Pacific. His one-time arch-enemy, Tank Thompson, saw some of the worst and survived."

"Where was that?"

"In China. He joined the Flying Tigers. Came home to marry Beth Shi and went back in as a Marine, island hopping all the way to Japan. How he lasted through that is a miracle."

"What about her brother, Lee, the table tennis champion?"

"He married Betty Devine after the war. Because of what she learned about his family, she had gone to China as a missionary, trying to help the people who had escaped the massacres at Nanking. She barely got out of there herself!"

"I know you were in Europe for a time, too. If you hadn't left, I wouldn't be here today!"

"Yes, and there would be no rolling ball clock at my birthday party."

He watched the arm swing down and scoop up another ball; the dial that records minutes rotated another notch. "I know Dad came to Jefferson City after graduating from Wesleyan, and that you arrived not long after. Did you recognize each other?"

"I didn't know he was the boy I'd talked with in St. Louis, at that little bookstore, but he knew who I was right away. He'd changed a lot since that meeting, matured, I guess. And his hair was longer, parted in the middle."

"That must have been interesting. After all, he'd written that song about you and kept the memory of you in his dreams."

I laughed. There were parts of our courtship I'd never told my children. And I wouldn't be giving him all the details today either. "I felt there was something familiar about him, but, as you say, I'd worked in hospitals in New Jersey and overseas. There had been men in my life, and this was a fresh start for me. I didn't make the connection for some weeks."

"But he was paying you special attention at work, wasn't he? He told me you were the prettiest girl at the lab."

"He did find ways to be where I was. And I didn't mind. He was quite handsome, you know!" Again, I gave a chuckle. He was a bit of a cut-up at work, and all the girls liked him.

"So, when did you learn you'd already met him?"

I smiled. "That's easy. The clock of our romance went back in motion when he put the photograph of me I'd sent him for the song contest on my desk."

The clock of my own life started running at that moment again, too, after the dark period of losing my father and Tony. And the months during which I saw all I ever want to of war.

Curtis smiled. "I've seen that picture. On the back Dad had written, 'Marry me.'"

$$\Omega$$

302

Dream On, My Heart

The night gently sighs; the breeze softly cries; my
heart is wak-ing from its dream of you. The

morn slow-ly comes; the stars quick-ly run, and my

heart is wak-ing from its dream of you.

Refrain

Dream on, my heart, dream of her; do not wake from your dream so de-

-vine. Dream on, my heart, dream of her; do not

304

SHORT QUOTE CREDITS

"My Old Flame," Sam Coslow

"Pennies from Heaven," Johnny Burke

"Let's Fall in Love," Harold Arlen, Ted Koehle

"God Bless America," Irving Berlin

"Lydia, the Tattooed Lady," Harold Arlen, Yip Harburg

"Moonglow", Eddie DeLange

Route 66 books by Michael Lund

Growing Up on Route 66 —Michael Lund (2000) ISBN 1-888725-31-1 Novel evoking fond memories of what it was like to grow up alongside "America's Highway" in 20th Century Missouri. (Trade paperback) 5x8 260 pp

Route 66 Kids —Michael Lund (2002) ISBN 1-888725-70-2 Sequel to *Growing Up on Route 66*, continuing memories of what it was like to grow up alongside "America's Highway" in 20th Century Missouri. (Trade paperback) 5x8 270 pp,

A Left-hander on Route 66--Michael Lund (2003) ISBN 1-888725-88-5. Twenty years after the fact, left-hander Hugh No one appeals a wrongful conviction that detoured him from "America's Main Street" and put him in jail. But revealing the details of the past and effecting a resolution of his case mean a dramatic rearrangement of his world, including troubled relationships with three women: Linda Roy, Patty Simpson, and Karen Murphy. (Trade paperback) 5x8 270 pp

Route 66 Spring-- Michael Lund (2004) ISBN: 1-888725-98-2. The lives of four young Missourians are changed when a bottle comes to the surface of one of the state's many natural springs. Inside is a letter written by a girl a dozen years after the end of the Civil War. Lucy Rivers Johns ' epistle contains a sad story of family failure and a powerful plea for help. This message from the last century crystallizes the individual frustrations of Janet Masters, Freddy Sills, Louis Clark, and Roberta Green, another group of

Route 66 kids. Their response to the past charts a bold path into the future, a path inspired by the Mother Road itself. (Trade paperback) 5x8 270 pp.

Miss Route 66--Michael Lund (2004) ISBN 1-888725-96-6. In the fourth novel of Michael Lund's Route 66 Novel Series, Susan Bell tells the story of her candidacy in Fairfield, Missouri's annual beauty contest. Now married and with teenage children in St. Louis, she recounts her youthful adventure in this small town along "America's Highway." At the same time, she plans a return to Fairfield in order to right injustices she feels were done to some young contestants in the Miss Route 66 Pageant. (Trade paperback) 5 X8, 260 pp, **Audio book** on 5 CD's ISBN 1-888725-12-5

Route 66 to Vietnam Michael Lund (2004) ISBN 1-59630-000-0 This novel takes characters from earlier works in the Route 66 Novel Series farther west than Los Angeles, official destination of the famous highway, Route 66. Mark Landon and Billy Rhodes find the values they grew up on challenged by America's role in Southeast Asia. But elements of their upbringing represented by the Mother Road also sustain them in ways they could never have anticipated. . (Trade paperback) 5 X8, 270 pp,.

Audio Book on CD—Route 66 to Vietnam ISBN: 1-59630-011-6 Michael Lund's fictional commentary from the viewpoint of a draftee. by Michael Lund unabridged 6 CD's --9 hours running time

Route 66 Chapel Michael Lund (2006) ISBN 1-59630-012-4 Route 66 Chapel, Michael Lund (2006) (Trade paperback) 5 X8, 260 pp. When the forces of progress threaten the foundation of small-town life—a small church—five senior citizens, a mysterious newcomer, and one young couple band together in an unlikely campaign to save it. The embattled meeting point of old and new is Route 66 Chapel, a building curiously linked to America's "Mother Road."

Route 66 Choir-- A Comedy (2010) Michael Lund ISBN 9781596300583   284 pp 5" x 8" In Route 66 Choir Stanley Measure takes early retirement just before September 11, 2001, and his impulsive decisions participate in an unraveling of confidence in the American way of life. His wife Felicia finds that everything she holds dear is in danger of coming apart: her marriage, her church, her business, and even her country. Who or what can orchestrate the recovery of harmony necessary to sustain the spirit of the Mother Road?

Route 66 Sweetheart (2011) ISBN 9781596300705 304pp 5"x8". This first of a novel series chronicles an American family during times of peace and war from 1915 to 2015. The first book, *Route 66 Sweetheart*, is set mostly in and around Rutherford, New Jersey, during the 1930s, where a young woman who traces her ancestry back to the early New World settlement of Nantucket comes to maturity during the Depression In the shadows of an emerging World War II.

Short Stories

How to NOT tell a War Story (2010) ISBN 9781596300798 (2012) 298pp 5"X8", A collection of stories about veterans who, though they were in a war, have no traditional war stories to tell. As they move into retirement forty years after the experiences, they begin to wonder if somehow there isn't something more to say about how their service affected their lives. Among other things, they come to appreciate the lovers, friends and family who helped them shape a new, post-war identity.

Michael Lund's five-volume novel series chronicles an American family during times of peace and war from 1915 to 2015. The first book, *Route 66 Sweetheart* (2011), is set mostly in and around Rutherford, New Jersey, during the 1930s. *Route 66 Dreamer* (2012) features the son of a Swedish immigrant who pursues his dreams of American success in Kansas and Missouri in the early 1940s. However, in both books some family members move away to distant countries and unexpected challenges.

The third volume, *Route 66 Looking-glass* (2013), will take place primarily in Missouri in 1965, but characters also travel far from home and familiar experiences. Book Four (2014) follows another generation of family members, this time from Missouri to Southeast Asia where many learn, sadly, "how to not tell a war story." In the final volume of the series (2015), the next generation travels to Europe and the Middle East to understand their identity in a multi-national community.